Enid Blyton's
MR MEDDLE'S
MUDDLES

"I wonder if bulls are pleased when they wag their tails," thought Meddle, feeling rather uncomfortable. "Dogs are, I know – but this bull doesn't look at all pleased as he wags his tail. Not one bit pleased. In fact, he looks awfully angry."

Meddle moved away a bit. The bull moved a little nearer and gave such an alarming snort that Meddle almost jumped out of his skin.

Also by Enid Blyton in Mammoth

Amelia Jane Again!
Amelia Jane Gets into Trouble!
Amelia Jane is Naughty Again!
Naughty Amelia Jane!
Tales of Betsy-May
Billy-Bob Tales
Bimbo and Topsy
The Blue Story Book
The Green Story Book
The Red Story Book
The Yellow Story Book
The Book of Brownies
The Book of Fairies
Family at Red Roofs
The Folk of the Faraway Tree
The Magic Faraway Tree
The Enchanted Wood
The Hidey Hole
Mr Meddle's Muddles
Mr Meddle's Mischief
Five Minute Tales
Ten Minute Tales
Fifteen Minute Tales
Twenty Minute Tales
Five O'Clock Tales
Six O'Clock Tales
Seven O'Clock Tales
Eight O'Clock Tales
The Adventures of Mr Pink-Whistle
Mr Pink-Whistle Interferes
The Put-Em-Rights
The Saucy Jane Family
The Seaside Family
Snowball the Pony
Those Dreadful Children
The Adventures of the Wishing-Chair
The Wishing-Chair Again

Enid Blyton's
MR MEDDLE'S
MUDDLES

MAMMOTH

First published by Newnes 1950
This edition published 1991 by Mammoth
an imprint of Reed Consumer Books Limited
Michelin House, 81 Fulham Road, London SW3 6RB
and Auckland, Melbourne, Singapore and Toronto

Reprinted 1993, 1994

Text copyright © 1950 Darrell Waters Limited

Enid Blyton's signature is a Registered Trade Mark
of Darrell Waters Limited

ISBN 0 7497 0812 3

A CIP catalogue record for this title
is available from the British Library

Printed and bound in Great Britain
by Cox & Wyman Ltd, Reading, Berkshire

CONTENTS

I

MISTER MEDDLE MAKES A MUDDLE

Once, when Meddle was staying with his Aunt Jemima, he broke one of her chairs. She was very cross about it.

"Meddle, you are very careless," she said. "I can't imagine how you broke that chair. It was quite strong."

"It fell over and broke itself," said Meddle.

"Somebody must have pushed it," said Aunt Jemima. "Well, it's not worth mending. It's got two legs and the back broken. I must go out this morning and buy another chair. And whilst I'm about it, I may as well get another little table for the kitchen corner there. It would be useful to put trays on. And I really need a new stool for my feet. I'll go and get them straight away."

"Shall I come with you and carry them

back for you, Aunt Jemima?" asked Meddle, anxious to make up for his carelessness.

"No, thank you," said his aunt. "You don't suppose I want them dropped all over the road and broken before they get home, do you? I shall tell the shop to send them when their van goes out this morning. You stay here and open the door when the van comes."

So Meddle stayed at home whilst his aunt went out. He stood at the window watching for the van to come. At last he heard a rumbling down the street and along came a heavy van. It stopped at the house next door, which was empty. Meddle tapped on the window.

"Hi!" he called. "This is the house. Hi, deliver the goods here, please. I am waiting for them."

The man got down from the van and looked doubtfully at Meddle. "Are you sure, sir?" he asked. "We were told to deliver at Number 8—and your house is 6."

"Of course I'm sure!" said Meddle, crossly. "I've stood here all the morning waiting for you. I'll give you a hand with the
things if you like."

"Well, my mate is here," said the man,
and he whistled to a man at the back of
the van. "This is the house," he called.
"I'll back the van a bit and then we'll
get the goods out."

So the big van was backed a little and

9

then the two men got to work. First they carried in a fine armchair.

"My word!" thought Meddle. "Aunt Jemima has got a much nicer chair than the one I broke. It's a beauty. I shall like to sit and snooze in that in the evening."

The men went back to the van and brought out a table. It was very big. Meddle stared at it in surprise. "Well, I quite thought Aunt Jemima would have bought a small one," he said to himself. "This will almost fill up the whole kitchen!"

"It's to go in the kitchen," he told the men, and he led the way. It really did almost fill up the little room!

The men went back to the van and came out with a bed, taken to pieces. Meddle stared at it. "Well, what's Aunt bought a bed for?" he wondered. "She didn't say anything about a bed. I wonder where it's to go. Well, there are only two bedrooms, and hers is the bigger, so it had better go in there!"

That wasn't the end of Meddle's surprise. The men brought a sofa out of the van, some more chairs, a sideboard, some stools, some carpets, another table and heaps of pictures!

"Aunt Jemima must have gone mad!" thought Meddle, telling the men to put the things here and there. "Yes, she must have gone quite mad! She set out to buy a chair, a little table, and a stool—and she seems to have bought a whole houseful of furniture! It's really very puzzling."

"Well, that's the lot, sir," said the men, and Meddle gave them a shilling. The van drove off and Meddle was left alone with all the furniture. He could really hardly move in the house, it was so crammed with chairs and tables and things!

Aunt Jemima came home at half-past twelve carrying a bag full of shopping. She let herself into the house and then stared in the greatest surprise at the hall. Usually there was a hall-stand there and nothing else. But now there were two chairs, a roll of carpet, and a small table!

"Meddle!" she called. "Meddle, what

are these things doing here?"

"Well, I didn't know where you wanted them to be put, Aunt," said Meddle. "Just tell me, and I'll take them wherever you like!"

"Meddle, I don't want them put anywhere!" cried his aunt. "I don't know anything about them."

"But you bought them, didn't you?" said Meddle, in surprise. "Aunt Jemima, do you feel all right? I must say I was rather astonished to find you had bought so much furniture this morning!"

"Are you mad, Meddle?" said his aunt, beginning to look at him in a way he didn't like at all. "I bought what I said I'd buy this morning—a chair, a little table, and a stool. Nothing else at all. And they can't be delivered till to-morrow. Now perhaps you will kindly tell me where all these things came from?"

"Aunt Jemima—Aunt Jemima—this is all very strange," said Meddle, staring round at the furniture. His aunt went into the sitting-room and looked in

12

amazement at everything there. She could
hardly move.

"Meddle, what in the world have you
been doing?" she said at last. "I know you

do the silliest things, but I can't think how you have managed to get all this furniture here like this, this morning. Where did it come from?"

"Two men brought it," said Meddle. He was beginning to feel most uncomfortable.

Just then a knock came at the door. Aunt Jemima opened it. A little woman stood outside, looking rather worried.

"I'm so sorry to trouble you," she said. "But we are moving in next door and our furniture van hasn't come along yet. I suppose you haven't seen it, have you?"

Then Aunt Jemima guessed everything. Silly old Meddle had taken in the furniture that should have gone next door! How exactly like him! If he could meddle, he would—and his meddles always made such muddles!

"I believe a dreadful mistake has been made," said Aunt Jemima. "I was out this morning and my stupid nephew has taken in your furniture here."

"Why—yes—it's my furniture!" cried

the little woman, staring round the hall in surprise. "Oh dear — and I've been waiting for it. The men are gone. Whatever shall I do?"

"Meddle shall carry it next door himself and put it wherever you want it," said Aunt Jemima firmly. "Meddle, do you hear me? It's no good your slinking off into the garden like that. Come back. You've made a fine old muddle and you're just going to put it right!"

"But I can't carry heavy furniture about!" cried poor Meddle, looking round at the chairs and tables in a fright.

"Well, you're going to," said his aunt. "Now begin right away, please, because I want to hang up my coat and hat and I can't possibly get into my bedroom until some of the things are taken from the landing!"

So poor old Meddle spent the rest of the day grunting and groaning under the heavy furniture, carrying it piece by piece into the house next door. How tired he was when the evening came! He sank down into a chair and sighed heavily.

"I'm not a bit sorry for you, Meddle," said his aunt. "Not a bit. You just won't learn sense. You didn't use your brains this morning, so you've had to use your arms and your legs and your back, and tire them out! Perhaps next time you will use your brains and save yourself a lot of trouble."

"I will!" said Meddle. "I certainly will!"

But, if I know Meddle, he certainly won't!

II

MISTER MEDDLE IS A SNOWMAN

One day Mister Meddle met his friend Jinks. Jinks was looking very cross, and Meddle was surprised.

"What's the matter, Jinks?" he asked.

"Someone's been taking the onions out of my garden shed," said Jinks. "I saw their footsteps in the snow this morning. I feel very cross."

"You should catch the thief, Jinks," said Meddle.

"All very well to say that, but he's gone," said Jinks.

"Well, he may come again. Can't you hide under a bush in the garden and watch for him?" asked Meddle.

"What, sit out there in the cold every frosty night, and have snow fall down my neck and the frost biting my fingers and toes? Don't be silly, Meddle," said Jinks, and he went off with his nose in the air.

Meddle stared after him. He didn't like

to be called silly. "Oh, all right, Jinks, if you're so high and mighty I won't try to help you," said Meddle, and he marched off too.

But on the way home a perfectly marvellous idea hopped into his head. He stopped and thought about it.

"I believe it's just the idea for catching the thief!" said Meddle. "If I pretend to be a snowman and stand still in the middle of Jinks's front garden, I shall be able to watch and see if the robber comes in. And he won't mind me at all, because he'll think I'm only a snowman. What a wonderful idea!"

He thought about it. How could he make himself like a snowman? He didn't think it would be very pleasant to cover himself with snow on such a cold night. No—he wouldn't have snow.

"I could wear my big new white mackintosh cape!" thought Meddle suddenly. "Of course! It would make me look like a snowman! What a splendid idea! And I could rub flour all over my face to make it white. And wear my own hat — snowmen always wear hats. They have sticks, too, so I can take my stick to hit the robber with."

Meddle felt very excited. He rushed home and got out his mackintosh. It covered him almost to the ground, so it would do very well.

"How pleased Jinks will be when I catch the robber for him!" thought Meddle.

"He'll be sorry he marched off with his nose in the air!"

That night Meddle crept down the road, with his mackintosh cape rolled up under his arm and his face white with flour. He didn't mean to put the mackintosh on until he came to Jinks's garden.

When he got there, there was no one about. So Meddle unrolled his big white cape and put it round his shoulders.

It fell almost to his feet. He kept his hat on, and he had a scarf round his neck to keep out the cold. Snowmen often had scarves.

Well, there he stood in Jinks's front garden, dressed in white, with his hat and scarf on—and a pipe in his mouth, too, though it wasn't lighted. He stood there feeling most important. Now let the robber come—and what a shock he would get!

Meddle stood there, and he stood there. It was cold. He began to shiver. He thought it would be a good idea to light his pipe. So he got out his matches, struck one and puffed at his pipe, lighting it up well.

Ah, that was better. He smoked his pipe gaily — and then he suddenly heard footsteps down the road. It was the village policeman passing by.

The policeman stood by Jinks's gate and sniffed. Funny, he could smell tobacco smoke — but there was nobody about at all. Then he caught sight of the glow in the bowl of Meddle's pipe. Goodness! Somebody was standing in Jinks's garden smoking — but there was no one there except the snowman.

"How can a snowman smoke a pipe?" wondered the policeman, puzzled. "How strange!"

He thought he would go into the garden and see what could be happening. So he opened the gate quietly and crept into the garden.

Now Meddle had no idea it was the village policeman. When he heard footsteps and then heard the gate open and someone coming inside, he at once thought it must be the robber!

"Ah!" he thought. "Now I'll give him a shock!"

So he walked forward two or three steps and yelled, "Stop, there!"

The policeman got a dreadful shock. He had never in his life before seen a snow-man that walked and talked. He stood still in fright, and couldn't say a word.

The snowman walked right up to him. The policeman simply couldn't bear it. He gave a yell and tore out of the gate and down the street. Meddle quite thought he must be the robber, and he tore after him, stumbling over his long white cape.

"Help! The snowman's after me! The snowman's after me!" yelled the frightened policeman. People came running out of their houses to see what was happening, and when they saw the snow-man rushing after the policeman, they were so frightened that they ran away too.

And soon Meddle found himself chasing quite a crowd of people. He began to enjoy himself. It was fun to make so many people run!

"Stop, stop!" he yelled. But nobody stopped. They ran on and on. The policeman got to the police station. He stumbled in, panting out that a snowman was chasing him — and all the other policemen put on their helmets and ran out to see. They were just in time to see the frightened people rushing past — and there was the snowman galloping after them!

One policeman put out his foot as

Meddle thundered past. Meddle tripped and fell over, rolling along the pavement. He was very angry.

"How dare you trip me up!" he yelled. "I was after the robber! Now he's escaped."

The policeman dragged Meddle into the police station. The frightened policeman, who had run away, was most astonished to see him.

"So you weren't a snowman after all!" he said. "You were dressed up in that white cape. Well, Mister Meddle, and what were you doing in Mister Jinks's garden, I should like to know? I suppose you weren't looking for his onions, by any chance?"

"How dare you say that," cried Meddle. "I was watching for the thief—and I thought you were the thief—and that's why I chased you!"

"Well, Mister Meddle, please don't go about pretending to be a snowman any more," said the head policeman. "You've caused enough trouble for one night, meddling like this. Anyway, Mister Jinks has locked up his shed and taken the key, so nobody can steal his onions again. You needn't bother yourself with the robber either — we caught him this evening, stealing somebody's leeks."

"Well, really! So all my trouble was for nothing!" said Meddle indignantly. "And I've torn my white cape and somebody's trodden on my hat — all for nothing. It's too bad."

"It's your own fault," said the policeman. "You shouldn't meddle!"

"Ho!" said Meddle haughtily, and off he went home, sticking his nose high in the air. He'll never learn, will he?

III

MISTER MEDDLE AND THE BULL

Did you ever hear about Mister Meddle and the bull? It's really rather funny.

Well, one day Mister Meddle got up feeling good. "I'd like to do a good deed to-day," he thought. "I'd like to help an old woman across the road, or carry a heavy parcel for someone, or jump into the river and save somebody from drowning. I feel good enough for all those things."

He went out to do his shopping as usual, and he looked about for a runaway horse that he could stop. But all his horses trotted along properly and not one ran away. So that was no good.

Then he walked by the river to see if anyone would fall in so that he could rescue them. But nobody did.

Then he looked about for anyone carrying a heavy parcel, but the only person he saw was Mr. Grumps, so he pretended not to notice he was carrying anything at all.

He waited about to see if any old ladies wanted to be helped over the road, but all the old ladies he saw seemed quite able to run across by themselves. So that wasn't any good either.

Mister Meddle was most disappointed. He went home by the fields, and in the distance he saw Farmer Barley, and he thought he would ask him if he could help him at all. The farmer was in the next field but one, so Mister Meddle opened the gate of the nearest field and shut it behind him, meaning to walk across to see the farmer.

The farmer heard the click of the gate and turned to look over the hedge to see who it was.

"I say!" began Meddle, shouting loudly. "Do you want . . ."

But Farmer Barley didn't wait to hear what Meddle said. He yelled over the hedge:

"Mind that bull!"

Meddle looked all round, but he couldn't see any bull. The farmer shouted again.

"Didn't you hear me telling you to mind that bull?"

"Now why does he want me to mind his bull?" wondered Meddle. "Oh — I suppose he wants to go home to his dinner or something, and would like me to mind the bull for him whilst he goes. Well, as I'm looking for something good to do, I'll do what he says."

Meddle yelled back to Farmer Barley, "All right. I'll mind the bull! Don't worry!"

"Right!" said the farmer, and went off down the field towards his farm. Meddle still couldn't see any bull, though he looked hard.

But the bull had seen him! It was in a little cluster of trees, and it didn't like the look of Meddle at all!

Meddle suddenly saw the bull looking at him. He decided that it didn't look a very kind animal.

"In fact, it looks rather fierce," thought Meddle. "Well, I'll mind it for the farmer, but I hope it won't try to run away, or anything, because I should just hate to try and bring it back."

The bull glared at Meddle and snorted down its nose.

"You needn't do that at me," said Meddle to the bull. "That's a rude noise to make at anyone minding you. Don't worry. I shan't come any nearer to you. I shall stay here and you can stay there."

But the bull didn't think the same as Meddle! It came out of the trees with a run and snorted at Meddle again, whisking its big tail up into the air.

"I wonder if bulls are pleased when they wag their tails," thought Meddle, feeling rather uncomfortable. "Dogs are, I know — but this bull doesn't look at all pleased as he wags his tail. Not one bit pleased. In fact, he looks awfully angry."

Meddle moved away a bit. The bull moved a little nearer and gave such an alarming snort that Meddle almost jumped out of his skin.

"You're making it very difficult for me to mind you!" he shouted to the bull. "Do behave yourself. I'm only minding you till the farmer comes back."

The bull made up his mind that he couldn't bear Meddle in his field one minute longer. So he snorted again and ran headlong at him, putting his head down in a horrid manner. Meddle took one look at the bull's horns and fled!

How he ran! He tore to the gate with the

bull after him, and got there just as the bull did. The bull tried to help him over the gate with his horns and tore Meddle's trousers, making a big hole. Meddle tumbled to the other side of the gate with a bump. The bull put his head over the top bar and snorted all over Meddle.

"You are a disgusting and most ungrateful animal," said Meddle angrily. "Look what you've done to my trousers! And all because I was doing a good deed and minding you for the farmer. Well — I'm not minding you any more, so you can just do what you like! I'm going to complain about you to the farmer!"

So Meddle marched off to the farmhouse, feeling very angry indeed. He rapped on the door and the farmer opened it.

"What's the matter?" he asked.

"Plenty!" said Meddle. "Look at my trousers — new last week, and that bull of yours chased me and tore them!"

"Well, I told you to mind him," said the farmer. "You should have got out of the field before he came for you."

"Well, I thought it would be better to mind him for you in the field," said Meddle. "That's what comes of trying to do you a good turn."

"What's all this about a good turn?" said the farmer, astonished. "I didn't want you to do me a good turn! I wanted you to get out of that field as quickly as possible before the bull turned on you. When I told you to *mind* the bull I meant you to look out that he didn't chase you!"

"Well, why didn't you say so?" said Meddle, in a rage. He turned to go and nearly fell over a fat pig.

"Mind that pig now—mind that pig!" cried the farmer.

Poor Meddle! He does get into trouble, doesn't he!

IV

MISTER MEDDLE HAS A SURPRISE

Mister Meddle once went to stay with his Aunt Jemima, who was very strict with him. She thought it did him good, and no doubt it did—but Meddle didn't like it at all.

His Aunt Jemima did a lot of good works. She went to read to sick people, and she took pies and soups to the poor. She knitted socks for the soldiers, and did everything she could to help other people.

When Meddle came to stay with her, she made him help her. "You can surely do a bit of knitting," she said. "It's easy enough."

But poor Meddle somehow managed to get the wool all tangled round him and lost his needles. "Are you trying to knit yourself as well as the wool?" asked his aunt crossly, as she untangled him.

"Perhaps it would be better if I took your pies and soups out?" said Meddle, thinking that it would be much easier to carry a basket than to knit a sock.

"Well, you can't make quite such a muddle with a pie as you can with wool, I suppose," said Aunt Jemima. "I am making a meat-pie to-morrow for poor old Mrs. Cook, who is in bed with a bad leg and can't do anything for herself. You shall come with me to see her, and carry the basket for me."

"All right, Aunt Jemima," said Meddle, with a sigh. "I'll come."

So the next day Aunt Jemima made a lovely round pie, with crust on it and a pretty pattern round the edge. She took it out of the oven, and showed it to Meddle.

"I wish we could have it for dinner," said Meddle longingly.

"Don't be greedy!" said his aunt. "Now just put it into that basket with a lid, Meddle. It's in the cupboard over there."

Meddle found the basket. It was oblong, and had a lid that shut down, so that whatever was inside was safe from cats or dogs. "Put the pie in, Meddle!" called his aunt. "And don't forget to shut the lid down. I'm going up to put on my hat. You can wait for me in the garden."

Meddle put the pie into the basket— but he forgot to shut down the lid. He went into the garden and put the basket down for a moment whilst he unpegged his scarf from the line. He felt to see if it was dry. It was, so he knotted it round his neck.

Now, whilst he was fiddling about with his scarf, a big blackbird flew down to the basket. It put its head on one side and looked at the pie. It looked good! The blackbird stood on the pie and pecked at the crust. Beaks and tails, it was delicious!

Meddle heard his aunt coming. He remembered that she told him to be sure to shut down the lid of the basket, and he hurriedly kicked it shut with his foot. He didn't see the blackbird inside! The surprised bird found itself shut in. It went on pecking at the pie, planning to fly out as soon as the lid was opened.

"Meddle! Aren't you ready?" cried Aunt Jemima. "Come along now. You always seem to keep me waiting."

Meddle picked up the basket and ran down the path to join his aunt. "Come along, come along!" she said. "We shall miss the bus."

"Oh, are we going to catch the bus?" said Meddle, pleased. He always liked a ride in the bus or the train. "Oh, good!"

He trotted along beside his aunt, swinging his basket, looking out for the bus. The blackbird inside didn't at all like being swung about like that. It gave a loud cheep. Meddle was most surprised.

He looked down at the basket. But the blackbird said no more for a while. Meddle and his aunt came to the bus-stop. The bus was not in sight so they both sat down on the seat.

Meddle put the basket on his knee, for he was afraid he might forget it if he put it down on the seat. The blackbird began pecking again at the crust. Peck, peck, peck!

Meddle had sharp ears. He listened to the peck-peck-peck in surprise. "Your pie does make a funny noise," he said to his aunt. She stared at him in surprise.

"Meddle, I do hope you're not in one of your silly moods this morning," she said to him sharply. "You know quite well that pies don't make a noise."

"Cheep-cheep!" said the blackbird. Meddle looked at the basket in astonishment. His aunt was a bit deaf, so she hadn't heard anything.

"Your pie is saying cheep-cheep," he told his aunt.

"That's nothing to what *you'll* be saying in a minute when I smack you hard," said his aunt crossly. "Telling me that pies say cheep-cheep! Hold your tongue, Meddle!"

The blackbird thought it would sing a

little song. So it swelled out its black throat, opened its yellow beak and trilled out a dear little tune:

"Tirra, tirra, ju-dy, ju-dee, dooit!"

"Aunt Jemima, I do wish you'd carry this pie yourself," said Meddle, beginning to feel alarmed. "It's beginning to sing now!"

"*Meddle!* If you don't stop telling me ridiculous things, I'll box your big ears!" said his aunt, in a real temper. "Pies that sing—what next?"

Luckily for Meddle, the bus came along at that moment and they got in. Meddle badly wanted to put the basket down on a seat, for he was beginning to be afraid of it now, but the bus was full, so he had to take the basket on his knee once more.

The blackbird was rather frightened by the noise of the bus, so it didn't cheep or sing for a while. But when the bus stopped, it gave a loud whistle. It was so loud that Aunt Jemima heard it. She turned to Meddle at once.

"Stop whistling! A bus is not the place to whistle in."

"I didn't whistle," said poor Meddle.

"Well, who did then?" said his aunt.

"The pie did," said Meddle. His aunt glared at him. "Meddle! Will you stop trying to be funny? First you tell me the pie cheeps—then you say it sings—and now you say it whistles! You'll be telling me it can fly next!"

Well, the blackbird took it into its head to flutter its wings and try to fly out of the basket at that moment. Meddle heard the fluttering wings in horror. Why, the pie was really doing what his aunt had said— it was flying round and round the basket. Meddle began to tremble like a jelly, and his aunt felt him shivering against her.

"Meddle, do keep still! You are making me feel all funny, shaking like that! Whatever is the matter with you this morning?"

"It's the pie," said poor Meddle. "It's flying round the basket now."

Aunt Jemima thought Meddle must be going mad. She was very glad when the

41

bus stopped and they got out. Mrs. Cook's house was quite near by. Meddle carried the basket there and thankfully put it on the table. Old Mrs. Cook was in bed and she stared greedily at the basket. She felt sure that something good was in there!

"Good morning, Mrs. Cook! I hope you are better!" said Aunt Jemima. "I've brought you a pie. I can't think what's the matter with Meddle this morning, because he keeps saying that my pie cheeps, and sings, and whistles — and flies!"

The blackbird whistled loudly again. Aunt Jemima thought it was Meddle, and she smacked him. "Now don't you dare to tell me that was the pie again!" she scolded. "Open the basket and put the pie on a plate."

But Meddle simply didn't dare to open the basket and touch that pie. He stood there, staring at his aunt, and she thought that really he must be going to be ill. So she opened the lid herself, in a rage.

And out flew the big blackbird and circled round her head! Aunt Jemima gave a scream. Mrs. Cook squealed for all she was worth—and Meddle tried to run for the door and fell headlong over a stool.

He got up and looked sternly at his aunt. "You bad woman! You cooked a blackbird in your pie! You bad woman! I suppose you remembered the twenty-four blackbirds that were baked in a pie—and you caught one and put it in! No wonder that pie sang and whistled and flew! Aunt Jemima, I'm *surprised* at you!"

And for once in a way his aunt hadn't a single word to say. She just couldn't make it out at all.

Meddle looked into the basket and then took out the pie. The bird had pecked an enormous hole in the crust. "Look there!" said Meddle, pointing to the hole. "That's the hole the bird pecked so that it could get out of the pie. I think you are a most unkind person, Aunt Jemima!"

He stalked out of the house and went home — and whenever his aunt scolded him after that, Meddle would stare hard at her and say, "Blackbirds! I haven't forgotten that, Aunt Jemima!"

And his Aunt Jemima wouldn't say a word more!

V

MISTER MEDDLE AND THE CHESTNUTS

Mister Meddle was very fond of roast chestnuts. He liked to make a little hole in them and put them down as close to the fire as he could without getting them burnt.

Then, when they were quite cooked through with the heat of the fire, he poked them away from the burning coal and let them cool in the fender. Then he peeled them, popped the delicious roasted nuts into his mouth and ate them.

But this year there were no chestnuts in the shops. Mister Meddle was very sad. He told his friend Jinky about it.

"You know, I'm going to miss my roast chestnuts very much," he said. "I just can't seem to buy any anywhere."

"Well, don't you know any trees that grow them?" asked Mister Jinky.

"I know lots of *horse*-chestnut trees,"

said Meddle. "You know—the kind we call 'conkers' when they fall to the ground and split open their prickly cases—but I don't know any trees that grow eating chestnuts. Do you?"

"Oh, yes," said Jinky. "I'll tell you. You know the Bluebell Wood, don't you?"

"Yes," said Meddle.

"Well, go right through it till you come to the big oak tree in the middle," said Jinky. "Then turn to the right, go down the little path there, and you'll soon come to two or three big eating-chestnut trees."

"How shall I know them?" asked Meddle. "They are not like horse-chestnuts, are they?"

"Not a bit," said Jinky. "You'll know them, my dear Meddle, because they are growing the eating chestnuts you love!"

"Are they in prickly cases like the conkers?" said Meddle.

"They are in cases, but much, much more prickly ones than the conkers," said Jinky. "What a lot of questions you ask, Meddle."

"Well, I want to be sure I don't make a mistake," said Meddle. "I'm always making mistakes—and I'm trying not to now."

Well, that afternoon Meddle took his biggest basket and set off to Bluebell Wood. He took the little path to the right when he came to the oak tree, and very soon he arrived at the three chestnut trees. Their leaves were quite different from the conker trees he knew — but Meddle couldn't

47

help knowing they were the right trees, because under them were scattered heaps and heaps of eating chestnuts, some still in their prickly brown cases, and others tumbled out, dark brown and shiny.

"My word, I shall have a lovely lot to take home and roast!" said Meddle, pleased. He began to gather them up and put them into his basket.

"What nice big ones there are!" thought Meddle. "And oh, my goodness me, look at *that* one!"

Now the one that Meddle was looking at wasn't a chestnut in a case at all. It was a small, brown, prickly hedgehog that had wandered up. As soon as it saw Meddle it had curled itself up tightly, so that it was nothing but a round ball of prickles. There it lay on the ground, perfectly still, looking for all the world like a very big chestnut-case, all prickly.

Meddle picked it up. The prickles hurt his fingers, so he soon dropped it into the basket. "What a giant chestnut must be inside this prickly case!" he thought.

"I'll open it when I get home, and see what kind of a chestnut there is there. Maybe there are two or three. What a find!"

He carried his basket home. The hedgehog didn't move at all. It was frightened. It knew that as long as it stayed tightly curled up, nobody could harm it. So there it lay in the basket, looking just like a big prickly chestnut.

When Meddle got home he was hungry. "I really think I will roast a few chestnuts at once," he said. "I feel as if I could eat a whole lot. I'll open this great big one first and see how many nuts there are inside it."

But, of course, he couldn't open it! The more he tried, the more tightly the hedgehog curled itself up. And Meddle pricked his fingers so badly that they began to bleed.

"You horrid chestnut!" said Meddle, crossly. "I'll just put you straight down beside the fire as you are — and you'll have to open then, and I'll get out your nuts!"

So down beside the fire went the hedgehog, along with a handful of nuts. Meddle sat down to watch them roast.

Now the hedgehog didn't like the fire at all. It was much too hot. It lay and thought what would be the best thing to do. It didn't want to be cooked. It didn't want to open itself and be caught. But as the fire felt hotter and hotter, the poor hedgehog knew there was only one thing to do—and that at once!

"I must crawl away, I really must!" it thought. So it opened out a little, put out its funny little snout, and began to crawl away from the hearth.

Meddle suddenly saw it. He thought he must be dreaming. He rubbed his eyes and looked again. The hedgehog was still crawling.

"My chestnut's walking!" yelled Meddle. Then he saw the little creature's nose, and he gave a yell.

"My chestnut's got a nose! It's got eyes! Goodness, gracious, it's grown legs, too!"

The hedgehog tried to get over the

hearthrug. Meddle gave another yell and rushed out of the house. He bumped into Jinky, and held on to him tight.

"*Now* what's the matter?" said Jinky in surprise.

"My big chestnut is walking on the hearthrug!" cried Meddle.

"Don't be silly," said Jinky.

"And it's got a nose," said Meddle, clinging to Jinky, for he really felt very frightened.

"You must be mad," said Jinky. "Who ever heard of a chestnut with a nose?"

"And it's got eyes and legs too," said poor Meddle. "Oh, Jinky, it must be magic. Oh, I don't like it."

"I'll come and see this peculiar chestnut," said Jinky. So he went into Meddle's house and looked around. But the hedgehog had heard him coming and had curled itself up tightly under a chair.

Jinky looked at it. "There it is!" said Meddle, pointing. "But how funny — it hasn't got eyes, or a nose or legs, any more."

Jinky knew at once that it was a hedgehog. How he grinned to himself! "We'll soon make it grow eyes and nose and legs again," he said. "Get me a saucer of bread and milk for your giant chestnut, Meddle."

"Bread and milk for a chestnut to eat!" said Meddle, in the greatest surprise. "Whatever are you talking about?"

"Go and get it," said Jinky. So Meddle went to his larder and soon came back with a saucer of bread and milk. Jinky set it down beside the tightly curled hedgehog. The hedgehog smelt the food. It uncurled itself. Out came a little nose.

Meddle gave a squeal. "Look! It's come alive again!"

The hedgehog went to the saucer on its short little legs and began to eat the bread and milk. Meddle watched in the greatest surprise, his eyes nearly falling out of his head.

When the hedgehog had finished the bread and milk, Jinky took out his handkerchief. He wrapped it round the little prickly creature, and lifted it up. The prickles were caught in the handkerchief and did not hurt him.

"If you don't want this giant chestnut, I'll have it," he said.

"Take it with pleasure!" cried Meddle.

"I don't want such a peculiar thing in my house. You seem to know what to do with it, anyway."

"Well, I've always liked hedgehogs," said Jinky with a grin. "They eat all the slugs and grubs in the garden! I never heard of anybody but gipsies trying to roast a hedgehog before! Another of your little mistakes, I'm afraid, Meddle!"

And off he went, grinning so broadly that his smile reached each of his ears. Well, well, well—what will old Meddle do next? I simply can't imagine, can you?

MISTER MEDDLE AND HIS AUNT'S CAT

Once Meddle went to stay with his Aunt Tabitha. He quite liked her, because she could make the most delicious chocolate puddings, and when she was in a good temper she used to make ice-creams that were almost too good to be true.

But what Meddle *didn't* like was his aunt's cat, Cinders. Cinders was a big black cat, with twenty sharp claws, and whiskers that stuck out straight from each side of his mouth.

"Cinders glares at me as if he simply hates me," Meddle complained.

"I'm not surprised," said Aunt Tabitha. "You've trodden on his tail at least six times this morning."

"Well, he shouldn't leave it laying about," said Meddle. "He should curl it round him like sensible cats do. He will leave it lying straight out. And I do think, Aunt Tabitha, that you should teach Cinders better manners. Do you know, he *spat* at me yesterday. Well, you've always told me that spitting is very, very rude."

"So it is," said his aunt, "but I'm not at all surprised at Cinders being rude to you. You stepped right into his bowl of milk and upset it. And what's more, you didn't bother to get a cloth and wipe it up."

"Well, that would have been a waste," said Meddle. "I didn't see why Cinders shouldn't lick up the milk off the floor himself, instead of my wiping it up. You're always tell *me* not to waste things."

"That's enough," said his aunt. "And don't come complaining to me any more about Cinders' behaviour. He doesn't complain about yours!"

"Well, if Cinders *dares* to complain about *me*, I'll – I'll – I'll . . .," began Meddle.

"You'll put him in the dustbin, I suppose," said Aunt Tabitha, crossly. "Well, you won't. If I hear of you daring to punish my dear, darling Cinders, I'll send you to bed for two days!"

So Meddle didn't dare to smack Cinders, however much he longed to. He just glared at him whenever he passed him, and Cinders glared back.

Now Meddle's Aunt Tabitha was very good about collecting paper for salvage. She kept a big sack into which every single bit of wastepaper was put, and when it was full, the dustman collected it. Meddle watched it getting fuller and fuller, and he was most interested in it. He put every bit of paper into it that he could.

"But, Meddle, *don't* put in to-day's paper before I've even read it!" said his aunt. "And, dear me, where is my writing pad? Surely to goodness you haven't put that in? Dear, dear, what a silly fellow you are. I don't know how I put up with you."

One day the sack really was full. Meddle felt sure it could be tied up and sent away. So he went to get some string from his aunt. Whilst he was gone, the cat jumped up on to the sack, and sniffed down into it. He always liked paper. It was soft and warm, and made a lovely noise. Cinders slipped himself right down into the sack, and scrabbled about happily. Then he made himself a nice cosy place and went to sleep.

When Meddle came back with the string he had no idea at all that Cinders had put himself into the sack. He tied up the neck firmly and then dragged the sack outside for the dustman to collect. Cinders woke up and felt most astonished at being dragged along like that. He stuck his claws out through the sacking and scratched Meddle's hand.

"Ow!" said Meddle, in pain. "There's something sharp in that sack. Aunt Tabitha must have put in her needle-case by mistake, or something. Horrid old sack!"

Meddle gave it a punch, and the cat yowled. That gave Meddle such a fright that he dropped the sack in a hurry by the dustbin, and fled indoors.

"Funny sort of sack," he thought, as he bathed his bleeding hand. "It scratches me, and then yowls. I'm glad it's going."

Now Cinders was most annoyed at not being able to get out of the sack. He jumped and scrabbled, he wriggled and struggled. He yowled and mewed, and made the sack sway about in the most alarming manner. When the cook next door came out into her yard, she was most astonished to see the sack behaving like this. She watched it in surprise.

The dustman came to collect it after a while, and the cook called to him: "You be careful of that sack! It's alive!"

"Ha, ha! Funny joke!" said the dustman, and hoisted the sack on to his shoulder. That was too much for Cinders. He let out a yowl like a siren going off, and dug all twenty claws through the sack into the dustman's shoulder. The man gave a yelp of surprise, and dropped the sack. Cinders leapt about inside it, and the sack jumped here and there in a most surprising manner.

"Well, I never saw a sack behaving like that before," said the dustman, scratching his head. "Yowling and scratching and jumping. I'll complain to the lady. I can't collect a sack that behaves like that."

So he knocked at the kitchen door and complained bitterly to Aunt Tabitha. She was most surprised.

"But it's only a sackful of paper," she said. "I know, because I saw every bit of paper that was put into it. Come, come, my man, don't be silly."

"Mee-ow, mee-ow!" said the sack, and did a few jumps round the yard.

"There you are," said the dustman. "You had better undo your sack, lady, and see what's the matter with it. It's my belief there's a tiger or a lion inside!"

"What nonsense!" said Aunt Tabitha. She fetched a knife and cut the string at the neck. Out jumped Cinders with another yowl, and a mass of bits of paper flew out after him. The dustman ran out of the back gate and didn't come back. The cook flew into her kitchen and slammed the door.

"Why, it's Cinders!" cried Aunt Tabitha, in surprise. "My dear, Darling Cinders! Meddle, Meddle, why did you tie up Cinders in the paper sack? You bad, wicked fellow, you wanted to get rid of Cinders, so you thought of sending him away in the sack! Oh, wait till I get you! *I'll* put you into a sack; so I will!"

Poor Meddle! He was well spanked with his aunt's hair-brush, and then he had to go to bed for two days. His Aunt Tabitha simply would not believe that he didn't know Cinders was in the sack.

Meddle wouldn't have minded staying in bed at all, for he was a lazy fellow—but

Cinders would sit on his window-sill and wash himself all the time. In between his washing he glared at Meddle out of his bright green eyes.

"And I daren't even throw my tooth-brush at him!" groaned Meddle. "Go away, Cinders, you nasty, glaring cat. Go away! I really will put you into a sack if you don't."

"No-eeow, you-eeow, won't-ee-ow," said Cinders, quite clearly. It really was rather hard luck for poor old Meddle, wasn't it?

VII

MISTER MEDDLE AND THE KANGAROO

Once upon a time there was a travelling circus that passed near to the town where Mister Meddle lived. Mister Meddle didn't know anything about it, because the circus didn't stop.

But, as it went by the town, the performing kangaroo escaped from its cage! Nobody saw it go. It found that its door hadn't been locked, so it just pushed it open and went out. It hopped right over the near-by hedge with one bound and then jumped in glee over three fields and a stream.

Now Mister Meddle was just out for his morning walk. He was trying to make up a poem that went like this—

> "The wind was soft and warm,
>   The sky was very blue,
>   The birds were singing sweet . . ."

Mister Meddle got as far as those three

lines and there he stuck. He just simply could NOT think of a fourth line.
He began again—

> "The wind was soft and warm,
> The sky was very blue,
> The birds were singing sweet . . .
> IS THAT A KANGAROO?"

Now Mister Meddle didn't mean the last line to rhyme like that, and it really sounded very funny. But he didn't think about its being funny—all he thought about was the very peculiar sight in front of him. Jumping down the field-path was a large kangaroo!

Mister Meddle was not used to meeting kangaroos in the fields. He stood still and stared at it.

"Now, I must think about this," said Mister Meddle. "Kangaroos don't live in this country. Therefore that can't be a kangaroo. On the other hand, it's not a rabbit or a hedgehog. And it does really look extremely like a kangaroo."

The kangaroo bounded nearer. It jumped right over a hedge and back again. Meddle began to feel a little scared. He didn't know how to treat kangaroos. Did you pat them like a dog? Or stroke them like a cat? Or prod them like a pig?

"Now I really MUST think about this," said Meddle firmly. "That *is* a kangaroo, but it can't be a real one. So I must be dreaming. Of course—that's what it is! I'm asleep and dreaming. It's only a dream kangaroo. Well, I'm not frightened of a dream kangaroo. Not a bit! Ho—I've only got to wake up and it will be gone."

The kangaroo bounded almost on top of Meddle, and stared at him in rather a fierce manner. Meddle stared back.

"Stare all you like!" he said to the kangaroo. "But let me tell you this— you're not real! Not a bit real. You're only a dream! My dream! Ha ha, ho ho!"

The kangaroo put its face near to Meddle's and made a horrid sort of noise. Meddle jumped back a little.

"If you do that sort of thing to me I'll wake up and then you'll be gone like a puff of smoke!" he said. "Do you want to be

gone? Just be careful, please. I don't like you very much, and I may wake up with a jump. Then you'll be gone for ever."

"Grr-rrr-rrr-rrr!" said the kangaroo, and put up its fists as if it were going to fight Meddle. It was a very clever kangaroo, and could box with its fists just like a man. It often boxed with its keeper, and it really thought that Meddle would enjoy boxing too.

But Meddle didn't like boxing at all. He stepped back a bit farther. The kangaroo followed.

"*Will* you keep away from me?" roared Meddle, getting angry. "You're a most annoying dream. I'll slap you if you keep following me. Now, I'm going to turn my back on you, and walk away. Maybe when I turn round you'll have changed into a pig or a cat or something, like things always do in dreams. So just look out!"

Meddle turned his back and walked away, hoping and hoping that the kangaroo would turn into a harmless mouse. But no sooner had he walked two steps than he felt a tremendous punch on his right shoulder. He nearly fell over.

He turned round in a rage. The kangaroo was dancing about all round him, aiming at him with its fists, enjoying itself very much. Meddle shouted at it.

"What do you want to punch me like that for? You might have woken me up! You know I'm asleep and dreaming, don't you? I wish I could wake up. You're a very horrid dream."

The kangaroo gave him another punch, right in his middle this time. Meddle bent over with a groan. "You horrid creature! You don't know how to play fair, even! Take that—and that."

Meddle hit out at the kangaroo, who was simply delighted. He gave Meddle such a punch that the poor man went right through the hedge and out at the other side! Two men were coming over the field there and they stared in great surprise at Meddle flying through the hedge.

"Do you usually come through hedges like that?" asked one of the men, at last.

"Of course not," said Meddle. "I'm having a very nasty dream, that's all. I can't imagine why you've come into my dream too. Really, I do wish I *could* wake up! I've already dreamt a kangaroo, and he keeps punching me."

"Dreamt a kangaroo!" cried one of the men. "Why, we are looking for a kangaroo! Where is he?"

"Oh, for goodness' sake don't call him!" said Meddle. "He's gone out of my dream for a moment and I really don't want him back."

"You must be mad," said one of the men. "You're not dreaming! You're wide awake."

"Now look here—I met a kangaroo just now, and I should never do that if I was awake," said Meddle. "I tell you, I'm dreaming. Pinch me, please. You can't feel pinches in dreams. Pinch me hard. I shan't feel it, and then you'll know I'm in a dream."

The men pinched Meddle as hard as they could. He gave a loud yell. "Ow! Don't! You're hurting me!"

"Well, there you are!" said the men. "You're not dreaming! Now—where's our kangaroo. He's escaped from our travelling circus."

Meddle stared at the men with his mouth wide open in surprise and horror. "Do you mean to say that was a real live kangaroo I saw?" he said at last. "I didn't dream him? Good gracious, I hit him! He might have eaten me up!"

The men laughed. "He wouldn't have done that," they said. "But you were mighty brave to hit him. He's very strong, and can be quite fierce. Look—here he comes, over the hedge!"

Sure enough, there was the kangaroo, leaping high over the hedge. He jumped to the men, and put his big arms round the one who was his keeper.

"Shake hands with this gentleman," the keeper said to the kangaroo. But Meddle wasn't going to have any more to do with kangaroos at all! He fled through the hedge again and tore home as fast as he could.

But you should have heard him boasting the next day!

"I was walking along making up a poem," he told his friends. "This was the poem—

> "The wind was soft and warm,
> The sky was very blue,
> The birds were singing sweet . . .
> IS THAT A KANGAROO?"

"But why did you put a kangaroo

suddenly into your poem?" asked his friends.

"Because there *was* one, an escaped one!" said Meddle. "Ah, you should have seen me! I went up to him. I ordered him to come with me, and when he wouldn't, I fought him. Slap, bang, I hit him hard. When his keepers came, I handed over the kangaroo to them at once. I shouldn't be surprised if they asked me to join their circus."

But Meddle didn't tell anyone at all that he had thought the kangaroo was a dream. Wasn't he funny?

VIII

MISTER MEDDLE MAKES A MISTAKE

Once Mister Meddle went out to a party at Mistress Fanny's. The streets were very dark, for there were no lamps lighted. Meddle took his torch with him—but, oh dear, what a nuisance! He had forgotten it was broken.

"Now I meant to get that mended this morning!" said Meddle. "How foolish I am! I do hope I shall get safely to Mistress Fanny's."

Just then Mr. Geeky went by, flashing his torch on the ground. Meddle was pleased.

"Hi, Mr. Geeky!" he called. "Are you going to Mistress Fanny's party? Can I come with you? My torch is broken."

"Come along then," said Mr. Geeky, and he flashed his torch at Mister Meddle. Meddle ran up to him and together they went along the road to Mistress Fanny's. It was fun to be going to a party.

It was a lovely party. There were plenty of good things to eat. There were three chocolate blanc-manges, six pink jellies, some egg sandwiches, and a fruit salad with a big jug of cream. Really, Meddle didn't know when he had enjoyed himself more!

There were games to play, and after a while Mistress Fanny cleared away the chairs, rolled up the carpet, and said they could dance. She set the gramophone going, and everybody began to dance.

At ten o'clock some of the guests began to go home. Meddle didn't. He always liked to stay till the very, very last.

But at twelve o'clock even *he* had to go, because there was nothing more left to eat and drink, and Mistress Fanny wanted to go to bed. So Meddle put on his hat and coat and looked round for Mr. Geeky.

But Mr. Geeky had gone home long before. "Oh dear!" said Meddle in dismay. "He had the torch! Mine is broken. I really can't go home in the dark."

"You'll have to, Meddle," said Mistress

Fanny at once. She didn't want to have
Meddle staying the night at her house.
She knew what an old meddler he was!

"Oh well, I suppose I shall find my way
all right," said Meddle. He said good-bye
to Mistress Fanny, and went carefully
down the path to the gate. He came to the
gate before he expected, and walked
straight into it. Oh, what a bruise he
would have on his knees to-morrow!

Meddle groaned and rubbed his knees. Then he stepped on to the pavement and made his way slowly up the road. He walked into a black cat, who spat at him and scratched his leg. He fell off the kerb at least three times, and sat down heavily in the gutter! Poor Meddle!

At last he came to his own street. At least, he *thought* it was! It wasn't really, but it was so dark that Meddle didn't know it was the wrong street. His house was the third one in his street, so Meddle counted the front gates he came to.

"One gate—two gates—three gates. This is my house! Good!"

He went in at the gate, and walked up the path to the front door. He took out his door-key.

It didn't fit at all! He could not make it turn in the lock—so the door remained shut and couldn't be opened. Meddle was very angry.

"What's the matter with the key?" he said. "Why doesn't it open the door? What a nuisance for it to go wrong at this time of night! Now what am I to do?"

He stood and thought hard. "I'd better go and see if the back window is open," he said. "I could get in that way."

So he stumbled round to the back, falling over a dustbin on the way. He came to the back window and tried to see if it would open. Yes! It would! Good! Now he could get in and go to bed.

So he climbed in through the window, and got into the kitchen. He felt about for matches and a candle, but he couldn't find them.

"Well, I really did think I had left my candle on the kitchen table," thought Meddle, vexed. "I suppose I didn't after all. Well, I must go up to bed without a light."

He found the stairs and tumbled up them. He came to the top, and tried to find the handle of his door. It didn't seem to be in the right place somehow. But at last he did find a door-handle, turned it, and went into the bedroom. The first thing he did was to walk straight into the bed!

"Now, the bed shouldn't be just here, surely!" said Meddle in astonishment. "It should be over in the corner. Who's been meddling with my room whilst I've been out? Just wait till I catch them! Putting my bed out in the middle of the room like this!"

He undressed himself in the dark, still grumbling. He felt round for the wash-stand, but that seemed to be in the wrong place too! Most extraordinary!

"*And* no water in the jug!" said Meddle, most surprised. "Well, I know I filled the jug this morning. I suppose the cat's been in and has drunk the whole lot. Just wait till I get hold of her! Drinking my washing water!"

At last he got into bed. He fell asleep almost at once, for he was very tired. He slept until the sun was quite high in the sky, and then he woke up and opened his eyes.

He was most astonished at what he saw. The walls were a bright pink. Meddle knew quite well that his usual wall-paper was pale green with a pattern of leaves.

He looked round the room. There was a pink carpet on the floor. Meddle knew he had only one green rug. There was an arm-chair with two cushions. Meddle's room had no arm-chair at all. The bed was wide and comfortable, and had on it a beautiful pink silk eiderdown, two pink blankets, and pink sheets.

Meddle looked at everything and

marvelled to see it. "This is magic," he said. "Real live magic! I go to bed in my own little green bedroom, and I wake up in a most beautiful pink one, with arm-chair and cushions, and the most comfortable bed I've ever slept in! Magic! Yes, wonderful magic!"

He lay in the soft bed and enjoyed himself. He felt hungry and wondered about breakfast. Perhaps there were servants in his changed house, who could cook for him a marvellous breakfast. Oooh! How fine that would be!

There was a bell near by in the wall. Meddle pressed it hard. It went "Ting-g-g-g-g-g!" very loudly indeed. Nobody came, though Meddle could quite well hear somebody moving about downstairs. He pressed the bell hard again—"Ting-g-g-g-g-g-g-g-g!"

Then he heard a voice exclaiming downstairs, "There's that bell again! There's nobody at the front door and nobody at the back. Whoever can be ringing the bell?"

"Ting-g-g-g-g-g-g!" Meddle rang it

again, feeling quite cross. There was the sound of footsteps coming upstairs. "I do believe it's my spare-room bell!" said a voice, and in came a big fat woman, with a red overall tied round her, and very fat cheeks.

Meddle stared at her. "Bring me some breakfast, please," he said.

"WELL!" said the woman in a most angry and astonished voice. "WELL! And what may *you* be doing here, I should like to know, in my best spare-room bed?"

"I don't know what you are talking about," said Meddle crossly. "Bring me some breakfast. I'm hungry."

"Well, hungry you'll have to be!" said the fat woman, and she tipped Meddle out of his warm bed. "How dare you sleep here! You wicked fellow! Get out of my house at once!"

"Madam!" said Meddle angrily, "How dare you treat me like this in my own house!" He climbed back into bed again. The fat woman at once tipped him out. She took hold of poor Meddle, who was dressed only in his best shirt, and walked him firmly to the top of the stairs. She gave him a push.

Down rolled Meddle, bumping from step to step. The woman ran down after him. She opened the front door and pushed him out into the garden.

"I'm going to get a policeman!" cried poor Mister Meddle. "I will *not* be turned out of my house like this." And off he rushed to find a policeman.

He ran up and down the streets for a long time before he could find Mr. Plod the policeman. Mr. Plod was surprised to see Mister Meddle in his best shirt and nothing else. And he was even more surprised to hear Meddle's story.

"You come along to my house and see this horrid woman," begged Meddle. So Mr. Plod went along to Mister Meddle's house, and as it was daylight, they went to the *right* house this time — Mister Meddle's own proper house.

And, of course, there was nobody there at all — no fat woman, no pink bedroom, no room with pink wall-paper! Mister Meddle couldn't believe his eyes.

"But where are my clothes?" he said. "I know I left them in the pink bedroom, Mr. Plod, because I saw them there this morning. Oh, Mr. Plod, where are my clothes?"

But Mr. Plod didn't know. He thought Mister Meddle was very silly. He left him and went down the road and up the next one. And there, on the pavement, he was very much surprised to see the rest of Meddle's clothes! The fat woman had thrown them out of the window after Mister Meddle, and there they were.

"Queerer and queerer," said Mr. Plod, and he took them back to Meddle. "Now don't you come along to me with any more silly stories," he said sternly, and he looked so cross that Meddle shivered and shook.

And to this day Meddle doesn't know what really happened. Isn't he an old silly, really?

MISTER MEDDLE MAKES ANOTHER MISTAKE

Once Mister Meddle felt rather gloomy, and he went about with such a long face that his friends teased him about it.

"Whatever is the matter?" they asked. "Have you lost a shilling and found sixpence?"

"Don't be silly," said Mister Meddle. "I am sad because I am bored."

"Look here, Meddle," said Gobo at once, "you haven't enough to do! That's what's the matter with *you*! You get a job of some kind—or go round helping people. That's the best cure for being bored or sad."

"Is it really?" said Mister Meddle. "Well, I'll do that then. I see that Biscuit, the grocer, wants another errand-boy. Perhaps I could take that job."

So off he went to Mr. Biscuit, and the grocer said yes, he could be an errand-boy.

"What have I to do?" asked Meddle, quite excited.

"Nothing much, except to take parcels round," said Biscuit. "This is Sam Quickly, my other errand-boy. He's a good lad. You can help him to-day for a start."

Well, as you know, Meddle was a muddler — and as Sam Quickly was just like his name, the two didn't get on very well together.

Sam did everything smartly and quickly

—but old Meddle fell over sacks, trod on spilt potatoes instead of picking them up, and covered himself with flour almost at once.

"Good gracious! You look like a miller!" said Sam with a giggle. "Here, take this parcel to Mrs. Brown's, and for goodness' sake dust yourself before you go!"

Meddle dusted himself so hard that the flour flew all over the place and Sam sneezed. Then Meddle took the parcel and went off to Mrs. Brown's.

But it was a very long way and before long Meddle began to puff and pant. When a bus came along he hopped into it.

"I shall wear out all my shoes if I walk so far," said Meddle, sitting down with a sigh. "How tired my feet are already!"

The bus was full. An old lady got in and glared at Meddle because he had put his parcel down beside him, so that there was hardly any room for her.

"Move that parcel!" she said sharply.

"Sorry," said Meddle, and he took up the parcel. He decided to sit on it, then there would be plenty of room. So he sat down on it. It made rather a peculiar noise, but that didn't worry Meddle. No, he just sat there happily.

Then he began to feel rather wet. He looked down at the seat and to his horror he found something bright yellow was dripping off the seat to the floor! The yolk of eggs! Good gracious — surely there weren't eggs in that parcel!

He got up in a hurry—and the parcel stuck to him! Meddle undid the paper quickly—and there, in the parcel, was a bag of twelve broken eggs, a bag of flour soaked with the eggs, a split bag of sugar, and half a pound of butter! The butter looked very strange indeed, for Meddle was quite heavy.

"Bother!" said Meddle. He picked up the spoilt parcel and got off the bus. He ran all the way back to Mr. Biscuit's and showed him the parcel.

"How was I to know there were eggs in it?" he said. "They have spoilt my trousers!"

"Serves you right," said Mr. Biscuit angrily. "What do I care about your trousers! Nothing at all! What I *do* care about is that you have spoilt Mrs. Brown's goods. Sam! Sam! Make up another parcel for Mrs. Brown and take it yourself. This poor, silly creature thinks parcels are to be sat on, not delivered."

Mister Meddle was angry. How dare Mr. Biscuit talk about him like that! He made up his mind to show him what he could do when he tried. Poor, silly creature, indeed!

"Make up two ounces of pepper for Mrs. Jones," said the grocer to Meddle. "And look sharp about it! It's in that drawer there."

Meddle went to the big drawer where the pepper was kept. It was lined with tin, and there was a scoop inside for measuring out the pepper.

Just as Meddle was taking up the scoop to measure the pepper, a large bluebottle came buzzing around. Now, Meddle simply hated bluebottles. He hated their buzz, and he hated their great fat bodies.

"I'll pepper you if you come near me!" said Meddle fiercely. "Keep away!"

The bluebottle at once flew round Meddle's head. "Zz-zz-zz-zz!" it said boldly. "Zz-zz-zz-zz!"

"All right!" said Meddle, in a rage. "I'll pepper you then!"

He threw a scoopful of pepper at the bluebottle. It flew off and came back again.

"Zz-zz-zz-zz! Zz-zz-zz-zz!"

"Get away, I tell you, get away!" yelled Meddle. He threw another lot of pepper at the bluebottle—and most unfortunately he didn't see Mr. Biscuit coming by, and the poor grocer found pepper flying all round him. He glared at Meddle and began to shout at him—and then he sneezed, and sneezed, and sneezed!

"You bad fellow . . ." he began, "you . . . a-tishoo! A-tish-oo! You bad . . . a-tishoo! Wait till I get you. A-tishoo!" Some customers came in and they began to sneeze too. How they sneezed! They sneezed so much that they had to go out of the shop without buying anything, and that made Mr. Biscuit crosser than ever. He gave the surprised Meddle a good slap.

"Stop playing about with the pepper!" he cried. "Go out and ask Sam to give you another job in the yard!"

So out went Meddle, sneezing hard himself. Sam was already back from Mrs. Brown's, and he looked in surprise at the sneezing Meddle.

"Got a cold?" he asked. "Good gracious, what a sneeze you've got—sounds like fireworks going off! Now come along and do a job of work. All these sacks of goods have got to be taken to the storehouse down the road, where Mr. Biscuit keeps a good many things."

Meddle looked at the sacks. Well, that seemed easy enough. He could carry a sack as well as anyone. Here goes! Up went a sack on his shoulder, and Meddle staggered off down the yard, out of the gate, and off to the shed down the road.

The sack was full of potatoes. It was very heavy. Meddle was glad to put it down when he reached the shed. He made up his mind that he wouldn't choose potatoes again—no, not he! He would choose a bag of sago or something that weighed much lighter.

Sam didn't seem to feel the weight of the sacks at all. He was a good and cheerful worker and he went up and down with the sacks, whistling merrily.

Meddle went round the sacks to feel which ones were the lightest of all. He chose a light one and went off with it. That was better! The next time he again chose a light sack, so that Sam had to take all the heavy ones.

"Look here," said Sam at last, "I'm carrying all the heavy ones and you're picking the light ones. That won't do!"

"All right. I'll take a heavy one this time," said Meddle, and he picked up a sack that he knew was very, very light indeed. It was full of new sponges, dry and light as feathers! But Meddle pretended that it was very heavy indeed, and groaned as he lifted the sack to his shoulder.

Sam knew the sack was full of dry sponges. He knew it wasn't heavy — Meddle was just pretending. Sam was about to shout at Meddle when something fell on his head — a big drop of rain. Then Sam grinned and said nothing at all. It was going to rain, was it? Well, let Meddle take the sponges then, and see what happened! He'd be rather surprised!

Meddle went off with the sack of sponges, smiling. Aha! He had the lightest sack of all, as light as a feather! It wouldn't take him long to run down the street with *that*!

It began to rain heavily. Thunder crashed overhead and the rain became so heavy that a little rivulet trickled down Meddle's nose and ran off the end.

Now you know what happens to your sponge when you fill it with water — it gets very heavy and very wet! Meddle had a whole *sackful* of sponges — and they began to get very wet indeed!

The wetter they got with the rain, the heavier they felt. Meddle was carrying a whole rain-storm in those sponges! He staggered along with the sack, which got heavier and heavier every minute. Meddle couldn't understand it!

"Now how can a sack change from light to heavy without my putting anything into it?" he said to himself. "I can't understand it!"

The rain fell more heavily, and the sponges in the sack soaked up the pelting drops and almost dragged Meddle down to the ground. He staggered along, his knees bending under him. Behind him came Sam Quickly, squealing with laughter, for he knew exactly what was happening.

At last the sponges were so heavy and

so big with rain that the sack could no longer hold them. It burst—and Meddle was buried under a pile of great wet sponges! When the wet, cold, slithery things slid over him, Meddle gave a yell.

"What is it—what is it? What have I been carrying? Frogs? Toads? Fish? Oh, they've come alive and they are out of the sack! Help, help!"

Meddle scrambled up and rushed home

97

in great fright. Sam Quickly laughed so much that he had to put his own sack down and wipe his eyes. Then he squeezed out the sponges and fetched a fresh sack for them.

"That's the last we'll see of our new errand-boy!" said Sam to himself. "And a good thing too!"

He was right. Meddle didn't go near Mr. Biscuit's again. He sat by the fire to dry his things and looked gloomily into the flames.

"Well, work's all right for some people," said Meddle to himself, "but it's no good for me. I've got too many brains to be an errand-boy!"

It's a great pity that Mr. Biscuit doesn't sell brains—if he did, Sam Quickly would buy some and deliver them at Meddle's house, I'm sure!

X

MISTER MEDDLE LOSES HIS TEMPER

Now once when Mister Meddle came home from doing his shopping, he found a cart outside his gate, and a man putting a whole lot of boxes and trunks in his front garden.

"Hey!" shouted Mister Meddle. "What are you putting those things in my garden for? Take them away."

"I'm putting them in the garden because I can't make anyone hear in the house," said the man, putting another box into the garden. "These things are labelled for your house. I can't get them into the house so I'm leaving them in the garden."

"Oh, no, you're not!" cried Meddle. "It's a mistake. These are not for me. I've ordered nothing from any shop. Take them out again!"

"I've spent all my time putting them in and I'm NOT going to take them out

99

again!" said the man, slamming down a large parrot-cage with an angry parrot inside.

"I say! I don't want that awful parrot!" yelled Mister Meddle, losing his temper. "Stop, stop! Don't put any more things in here."

"That's the last!" said the man, and he put down a large round hat-box. "Good day to you!"

He climbed up to his seat, clicked to his old brown horse, and clip-clopped off down the street. Meddle was so angry that he went purple in the face. He caught up the hat-box and threw it after the man.

It rolled down the street after him. It broke open, and three big hats with red, pink, and yellow flowers on them shot out of the box into the gutter.

"Good!" said Meddle fiercely. "Stay there, hats!"

He looked at all the things messing up his garden.

The parrot glared at him and he glared back at the parrot.

The big bird unexpectedly began to sing, swaying to and fro on its perch,

"Yankee doodle came to town,
Upon a little pony!"

sang the parrot. Then he broke off to look rudely at Meddle, and said. "Go and brush your hair! Go and brush your hair!"

"Now look here," said Meddle in a fine

temper, "I won't have parrots telling me what to do! Be quiet! Brush your own hair!"

"Yankee doodle, go and wash your face!" said the parrot, and then it put back its head and laughed with a loud screech. Meddle went to the cage, took hold of it, and carried it to the gate. He threw it over the gate into the road. Crash! The cage hit the ground, the parrot let out a squawk, and then began to call Meddle all kinds of rude names.

"Well, what a morning, what a morning!" shouted Meddle in a fury. "Things all over my garden! Parrots telling me to wash my face! Hats in the gutter! I won't have it!"

He caught up a small box and sent that flying over the hedge. Smash! It hit the ground, burst open, and spilt white stockings all over the road.

"White stockings!" said Meddle in amazement. "Who in the world wears white stockings now! Well, here goes!"

He sent another box flying over the

hedge. It spilt open and soap, scent, tooth-brushes, creams, hair-pins, and all kinds of things burst out of it. Meddle giggled. It was funny to see such an odd crowd of things in the road. Then he went quite mad and threw everything else over the hedge too.

Bang! That was a big trunk. Crash! That was a wooden box. Smash! That was a bag with something breakable inside. My word, what a game!

"That'll teach people to pile up my garden with things that don't belong to me!" cried Meddle, thoroughly enjoying himself.

By this time quite a crowd had come along and every one was watching Meddle in greatest surprise.

"Help yourselves!" cried Meddle, looking over the gate. "They don't belong to me! Help yourselves!"

At this moment a cab drew up near by and a rather fat old woman looked out. She saw Meddle and waved to him.

"Meddle, Meddle! I'm so pleased to see you! I hope you didn't forget I was coming to-day to stay with you. You wrote me such a nice letter — but you're so forgetful, aren't you!"

Meddle stared at the large old lady getting out of the cab, with a big umbrella and red bag.

"AUNT JEMIMA!" he cried. "Ohhhhh-hhhhhhh!"

Aunt Jemima looked round and saw the crowd of people. She saw the trunks, bags, and boxes in the road, spilt and bursting. She saw the parrot's cage, all on one side with the parrot squawking for all he was worth:

"Go and clean your teeth! Go and clean your teeth!"

"My parrot!" screamed Aunt Jemima. "Who put him out there in the road, all on one side?"

"Meddle threw him over the gate," said someone.

"THREW HIM OVER THE GATE!" said Aunt Jemima in a truly dreadful voice. "And who threw all these boxes and trunks of mine out here?"

"Meddle did!" shouted everyone.

"MEDDLE! Do you mean to say that you threw all my goods into the road like this?" said his Aunt Jemima, her red face going even redder.

"I forgot you were c-c-c-coming, Aunt Jemima," stammered Meddle. "A man brought these things into my garden when I was out, and I d-d-d-d-didn't think of them being yours. I lost my t-t-t-temper and threw them over the hedge."

"Meddle, I'm going to lose my temper too," said Aunt Jemima. "When you were a naughty, meddlesome little boy, I had to spank you — and, Meddle, I feel that's what I'm going to do now. Come here!"

But Meddle didn't come. He went! Down the street he went like lightning.

His Aunt Jemima snorted.

"Well, I can wait till he comes back," she said. "Cabman, pick up all these things and take them into this house for me. I'll take the parrot, poor darling."

"Go and clean your shoes! Go and clean your shoes!" said the parrot softly, and tried to rub its head against Aunt Jemima's fingers.

"You clever thing," said Aunt Jemima. "Wait till I get hold of Meddle. I'll teach him to throw parrots into the road. Lost his temper indeed! Wait till he sees me lose mine! He'll get a fine shock!"

Poor Meddle! He doesn't dare to go home —and Aunt Jemima is quite determined to stay till he does. So what's going to happen, do you think?

XI

MISTER MEDDLE'S UMBRELLA

When Mister Meddle went to stay with his Aunt Jemima, she was very strict with him. She made him put on galoshes when it was wet, and a hat when it was sunny, and a scarf round his throat when the wind was cold.

"I wish you wouldn't fuss!" Meddle kept saying. "Aunt Jemima, I wish you wouldn't FUSS!"

"Meddle, you are so silly that I'm sure I don't know what would happen to you if I didn't fuss," said his aunt. "I am *not* going to have you in bed with colds while you are staying here — so I am going to fuss all I like, and you will have to do as you are told."

Now if there was one thing more than another that Meddle hated, it was taking an umbrella out with him. He simply couldn't bear it.

"If I have to carry an umbrella it's a

perfect nuisance!" he said. "It gets between my ankles and trips me up. It digs itself into people as I pass them, and they get angry with me. I just can't bear an umbrella."

"Well, my dear Meddle, you'll have to take one this afternoon when you go out, because it's simply pouring with rain!" said his aunt firmly. "Look at it—pouring cats and dogs."

"I wish it really *would* pour cats and dogs," said Meddle. "I've always wanted to see that, and I never have. I shan't go out this afternoon, Aunt Jemima, if you make me take an umbrella."

"Very well," said his aunt. "Then you can't call at the book shop and get your *Sunny Stories*."

"Oh, I simply *must* have that," said Meddle. "Why, I might be in the book this week."

Well, it was still raining that afternoon when Meddle put his coat on, and told Aunt Jemima he was going out. His aunt went to the hall-stand and fetched her umbrella. It was a fat red one, and had a bright red, crooked handle. She gave it to him.

"You'll get wet through if you don't take this," she said. "Go along now. Hurry up!"

"Bother!" said Meddle. "Bother, bother, bother. I do so hate umbrellas."

"Meddle, if you don't take it, you don't go out!" said Aunt Jemima. So Meddle took it, and went down the garden path. He began thinking about a story he was going to write. It was to be about a soldier who was very brave.

"He shall have a sword," said Meddle to himself. "An enormous sword. And he will use it like this—slash, slash, poke, poke, slash, slash!"

Meddle began to slash about with the umbrella as if it were a sword. My, he did feel grand. People stared at him in surprise as they passed, but Meddle didn't even see them.

"My soldier shall fight well!" he cried. "Slash, slash!"

He nearly knocked old Mrs. Jinks's hat off her head, and she scurried away in fright. Meddle went all the way to the bookshop in the pouring rain, pretending that the umbrella was a sword. He didn't even put it up. He soon was quite soaked, and the rain dripped down his neck.

So, of course, when he got home again, his coat was dripping and his hair was so wet that it looked dreadful.

"Meddle! Didn't you put up your umbrella?" cried his aunt angrily. "Oh, you silly creature! What's the use of taking out an umbrella if you don't put it up? Now you will get a dreadful cold."

"A-tish-oo!" said Meddle, with a sneeze. And the next day he was in bed, feeling very bad.

Well, when he was up, and wanted to go out for a walk, his Aunt Jemima looked up at the sky. "Meddle," she said, "it looks like rain. I don't think I can trust you to go out. You'll only get wet again."

"Aunt Jemima, if only you'll let me go out and buy a bottle of boiled sweets,

I promise I'll take an umbrella," said Meddle.

"But will you put it up?" asked his aunt. "You took an umbrella last time, but you didn't put it up. And what's the use of that? Last time you said your umbrella was a sword. This time you may pretend it's a lamp-post or something."

Well, Meddle got his way. He took the fat red umbrella out of the hall-stand

and went off. It wasn't raining, but after a little some drops began to fall. Meddle was busy putting his hand into the bag to get out a nice red sweet, and he was cross.

"Stupid rain!" he said. "Well, I promised my aunt to put up the umbrella, so I must."

Meddle held up his umbrella above his head, but he didn't put it up! He just held it up like a stick, without opening the umbrella at all. He was so busy with his sweets that he forgot that an umbrella must be opened when it is held up. So there he was, going down the road, getting wetter and wetter, his umbrella held un-opened above his head.

"Well, well," said Meddle to himself. "What's the use of an umbrella, after all, I'd like to know? I'm getting just as wet as if I'd not taken one with me at all. Splash, splash, splash, the rain comes down — and I'm getting soaked."

Now Aunt Jemima was watching for Meddle when he came home — and when she saw him walking up the path with his umbrella held like a stick over his head, she was really very angry. Meddle saw her frowning and he was puzzled.

"Now what's the matter, Aunt?" he cried, as he walked up the path and saw her looking out of the window. "I took the umbrella, didn't I? And I put it up, didn't I? But what's the use—I'm just as wet as ever!"

"My dear Meddle, you might as well take a peastick to hold over your head as an umbrella, if you don't bother to put it up," said his aunt. "Look up and see your umbrella."

So Meddle looked up, and saw that he had forgotten to open the umbrella, and he felt rather foolish. "Dear me," he said. "I've been rather silly."

"You'll have a cold to-morrow," said Aunt Jemima.

"A-tish-oo!" said Meddle. And, of course, he was in bed with a cold the very next day.

Well, well. Aunt Jemima was very

cross and not a bit nice to Meddle. When he was up again, she spoke to him very sternly.

"Meddle, every time you go out in future you will take an umbrella with you," she said. "And you will practise putting it up and down, up and down, before you go out. Then perhaps you will remember that an umbrella is meant to be opened when it is in use."

So Meddle practised putting the umbrella up and down, and opened and shut it a dozen times before he went out. The cat hated it. It was a great shock to her whenever Meddle suddenly opened the umbrella just in front of her.

When Meddle's cold was well enough for him to go out, his aunt made him take the umbrella with him.

"But it isn't raining!" said Meddle. "No, Aunt, I'd look silly."

"You'll look a lot sillier if you get a third cold, and miss your birthday party," said Aunt Jemima. "Take the umbrella, and don't make a fuss, Meddle."

So Meddle took it with him, though the sun was shining brightly. He went to visit his friend Gobo, and he sat and talked to him for a long time. And, of course, when he left to go home, he quite forgot to take the umbrella with him. He left it behind in Gobo's hall-stand!

And when he was almost home the rain

came down. How it poured! You should have seen it. Meddle got quite a shock when he felt the big raindrops stinging his face.

"Ha! Good thing I took an umbrella with me!" he said. "A very good thing indeed. I'll put it up."

But the umbrella wasn't there to put up. Meddle stared all round as if he thought the umbrella would come walking up. But of course it didn't.

"Bother!" said Meddle. "Where's it gone? I know I had it when I left home. How can I put an umbrella up if it isn't here? My goodness! What will Aunt Jemima say when she sees me coming home in the rain without the umbrella? I wonder if she's looking out of the window. I won't peep and see in case she is. I'll run all the way back to Gobo's and see if I've left the umbrella there!"

If only Meddle had looked he would have seen his aunt knocking at the window to tell him to run quickly up the garden path and come in out of the rain!

Instead of that, he ran down the road again, and went all the way back to Gobo's with the rain pouring down on him. How wet he got! He dripped like a piece of seaweed.

By the time he got to Gobo's he was wet through and shivering. He banged at the door. Gobo opened it.

"I've come back for my umbrella before I get wet," said Meddle.

"You silly! You're soaked already," said Gobo. "As for your umbrella, I've sent Mrs. Gobo to your aunt's with it. You must have missed her. I can't lend you one because I haven't one at the moment. My goodness, won't you get wet!"

So Meddle had to run back in the rain without an umbrella at all, and his shoes went squelch, squelch, squelch, and his coat went drip, drip, drip.

How angry his Aunt Jemima was when he came in. "Meddle! I send you out with an umbrella, and you come home in the pouring rain without it, and I knock at the window to tell you to come in, and you run off down the road again, and then Mrs. Gobo comes in with your umbrella, and you come home again as wet as a sponge. You'll get a very bad cold."

"A-tish-oo!" said Meddle at once. "A-tish-oo! I must go and get a hanky!"

And, of course, he was in bed with a bad cold the next day and missed his birthday party after all! Now he is packing up to go home because his aunt says she won't keep him any longer. Do you know what she gave him for a birthday present? Guess! An umbrella—and the handle is a donkey's head.

"I chose a donkey because I really thought it would suit you well," said Aunt Jemima.

But I expect he will leave it in the bus, don't you?

XII

MISTER MEDDLE DOES A BIT OF GOOD

Once there came a magician to Meddle's village. He was very clever, and knew a great deal of magic. His name was Sneaky, and he was just like his name.

He was not a nice person. He was horrid to everybody, and they couldn't be horrid back, because they were afraid of him. They stayed in their houses when Sneaky came by, because they were so afraid he might take them to be his servants.

But, of course Meddle didn't stay in *his* house. Oh no!—he was far too curious about Sneaky. He longed to see what he was like. So when he knew that the magician was coming down the road, Meddle hopped out of his front door and squeezed himself inside a bush, so that he might peep out at Sneaky.

Sneaky wore very soft shoes that made no sound. Meddle couldn't hear him coming at all. "I must peep out and see if he has gone by," said Meddle at last. So he poked out his head—and just at that very moment Sneaky came by! He saw Meddle peeping out of the bush and he stopped and grinned.

"Ho! Spying on me! This won't do, my dear fellow, this won't do!"

"I'm s-s-s-s-orry!" said Meddle, shivering in his shoes. "I j-j-j-just wanted to s-s-s-see what you were l-l-l-like!"

"Oh, you wanted to see what I was like, did you?" said Sneaky. "Well, you just come home with me, and you'll soon see what I am like! I need a servant."

And to Meddle's dismay Sneaky reached out a long arm, picked him out of the bush, tucked him under his arm like a parcel and went off with him.

"Well, it serves Meddle right," said everyone, peeping from their windows. "He is always prying and meddling!"

Poor Meddle! He didn't like being the magician's servant at all. He wasn't very good at cooking. He wasn't very good at cleaning. He didn't remember anything he was told, and he was always poking his nose into the magician's books and spells.

"One day you'll leave your nose behind you, if you poke it into any more of my magic," said Sneaky angrily, when he found Meddle reading one of his magic books. "Go about your work. Clean my broomsticks to-day, and all the furniture too. It looks dreadful! Look at those smears! Look at those stains!"

"Y-y-y-yes, sir," said Meddle. "B-b-but I haven't any more p-p-p-polish."

"What a nuisance you are!" said Sneaky. "Always wanting some more of this, and some more of that. I will give you some polish to-day—and you must make it last for a whole week."

Sneaky went to a cupboard. He took out two tins. One was blue and one was green.

"Now listen carefully," he said sternly to Meddle. "This blue tin is for my broomsticks. It is a fly-away polish, and has magic in it, so that when I want to use my broomsticks to fly away on, they will go smoothly and swiftly through the air. And this polish, in the green tin, is a good bright polish for the furniture. Now go away and work hard."

"Yes, sir," said Meddle, and he took the tins of polish. He went to the kitchen. He sighed deeply. He hated polishing. He looked at the clock—four o'clock, tea-time!

"I really must have a cup of tea first," said Meddle. Just then he heard the front door bang, and he ran to the window. "Ha! There's old Sneaky going out! Good! Now I can have a cup of tea in peace."

He made himself a pot of tea. He sat back on a chair, put his feet on a stool, and took up his cup. Ah, this was nice — almost like being at home!

But just then he heard the sound of a key being slid into a lock — Sneaky was back again already! Meddle leapt up in a great hurry, spilt the tea all down himself, and rushed to get his polishing cloths. If Sneaky found him lazing instead of polishing, how angry he would be!

Meddle opened the two tins of polish. He

stole quietly into the dining-room, where Sneaky kept his magic broomsticks. Then he looked at the tins of polish.

"Goodness!" said Meddle, scratching his head. "Now which was which? Was the blue tin the fly-away polish, or the green?"

He simply *couldn't* remember. He didn't dare to go and ask. He stood there and stared at both tins.

"Well, *I* think Sneaky said the green polish was for his broomsticks, and the blue polish was for the furniture," said Meddle at last. "I'll do the broomsticks first."

He began to polish the broomsticks with the green polish. They shone and glittered. Meddle did all six of the broomsticks, and then turned to the furniture. He dabbed his cloth into the tin of blue polish. It was the fly-away polish, of course, but Meddle didn't think it was.

"I'll polish Sneaky's oak chair first," said Meddle to himself. "That's about the most important piece of furniture in the room."

So he began to polish the big arm-chair with the blue polish. My word, how that chair shone and gleamed! It was marvellous polish. And it was magic too — for whoever sat down in that chair would now fly away in it, goodness knew where.

"Oooh, I'm tired," said Meddle at last. "My arm aches. I must have a little rest. I'll pretend to be Sneaky and sit down in his chair. How grand I shall feel!"

Meddle was just about to sit down in Sneaky's chair, when the magician himself came into the room. How he glared at Meddle!

"What! You are daring to sit in my chair!" he cried. "Get out at once!"

He pushed Meddle so hard that the poor fellow went spinning into a corner, and fell over all the broomsticks there. They tumbled across him with a clatter.

"Ha ha!" laughed Sneaky, sitting down hard in his chair. "How funny you look, Meddle!"

But his laughter soon stopped, and a frightened look came on his face. His chair was rising into the air! "Hi! What's this? Stop, stop!" yelled Sneaky. But the chair didn't stop. It flew up to the ceiling. Bang! It made a hole there! It flew through the hole, up, up to the roof!

"You wicked meddler, you've polished my chair with the fly-away polish!" yelled Sneaky in a rage. "Wait till I jump out and catch you!"

But it was too late for him to jump out. Crash! The chair flew through the roof, and a shower of tiles fell down. Meddle stared in the greatest surprise. He ran to the door and looked upwards. There was Sneaky flying away in the old oak chair —up, up, up to the clouds! He got smaller and smaller, the farther he went.

"Ooooh," said Meddle, hardly believing his eyes. He sat down on the grass and wiped his forehead. "Ooooooh. He's gone. Simply gone. Just like that! And all because I used the wrong polish. Well, well, well! It seems as if it's a good thing to be silly sometimes!"

The folk in Meddle's village saw the

curious sight of Sneaky flying through
the roof of his house, away up to the
sky. They came running to Sneaky's
house, and there they saw Meddle sitting
on the grass.

"What's happened? What's happened?"
they cried.

"Well, you see, I polished Sneaky's
chair with the wrong polish," explained
Meddle. "I used the fly-away polish
instead of the furniture polish. I am
always so foolish."

"Why, Meddle, that was the cleverest thing you've ever done!" cried everyone.

"But I didn't mean to be clever," said Meddle honestly. "It was a mistake!"

"Good old Meddle, fine old Meddle!" cried everyone, and they all crowded round him and shook hands.

"Come to tea with me to-morrow," said one.

"Come and have some of my ripe plums," said another.

"Come and have a cup of cocoa with me," said a third.

Meddle was most astonished. He wasn't used to being made a fuss of. He liked it. It was nice.

"Thank you, kind friends," he said. "I think that now I've done *one* clever thing, I may perhaps be cleverer in the future. Anyway, I'll try!"

So he's trying, and not getting on so badly either. I'll be sure and tell you if he starts meddling and getting into trouble again.

MISTER MEDDLE AND HIS HANDKERCHIEF

When Meddle went to stay with his Aunt Jemima he always had to be on his best behaviour. One of the things he had to be careful about was coughing.

"*Always* cough into your hanky, Meddle," his aunt would say. "Decent people always do — nasty people don't."

"Oh," said Meddle, thinking that his aunt must often have thought him a nasty person. "Well, I'll try, Aunt Jemima. But I haven't always a hanky with me."

"Well, you must put a hanky into your pocket every morning," said his aunt.

"I haven't got a pocket," said Meddle. "You sewed them all up because you said I kept putting my hands into them."

"Well, pin a hanky to the front of you," said his aunt.

"No, certainly not," said Meddle. "People would laugh when they saw me."

"Well, put your hanky into the top of your stocking then, or down your neck—anywhere you can get it if you feel you are going to cough," said his aunt.

So Meddle fetched a hanky, and put it down his neck, just under the top of his blue vest. Now he could easily get it if he coughed.

He didn't cough all the morning. He didn't sneeze, either. That afternoon his Aunt Jemima said: "Meddle, I am going out to a meeting this afternoon. It is a meeting of some very, very good people, who are going to give money so that we may teach poor little children their manners. Now, you just show what nice manners *you* have—hand round the cakes at tea—and put chairs for everyone—and answer nicely when you are spoken to."

"I don't feel I have nice enough manners for a meeting like that," said Meddle. But his aunt would not let him stay at home. She took him with her, and he had to go. He was afraid of his Aunt Jemima because she always said Meddle was still young enough to be spanked.

So he went. He tried to behave nicely. He put chairs for everyone. He looked at the cakes on the tea-table and decided that he would hand a few to himself as well as to other people. He answered very nicely when he was spoken to.

"Now, there's a very nicely behaved nephew of yours," everyone said to Aunt Jemima. "You must be proud of him. If

133

only we could have the little children in far-off countires brought up like Meddle, what a wonderful thing it would be!"

Everything went well until tea-time. Then Meddle began to hand round the cakes as he had been told. Then he was asked to take cups of tea to people. He took a cup in one hand and a cup in the other.

He was just walking across the room when he felt a sneeze or cough coming. He didn't know which. It might quite well be both.

"My hanky!" thought Meddle in dismay. "Did I bring one? Yes, thank goodness I did. I put it down the top of my vest, didn't I? Oh, I shall burst if I don't sneeze or cough soon."

He had to put down the cups of tea quickly. He pushed one into Mrs. Plumpy's lap, and it spilt all over her new purple dress. He shot the other at Miss Skinny, and it scalded her hand. They both squealed loudly.

Everyone looked at Meddle, which was a great pity, because Meddle was doing surprising things. He was trying to find his hanky — and it wasn't where he had put it! He was feeling about in his vest, but there was no hanky there!

"Meddle! Whatever are you doing?" said his Aunt Jemima in horror. "Have you got a mouse down your front, or what?"

Meddle couldn't answer, because he was trying to keep his cough inside him till he found his hanky. He looked at his aunt, and his face went red and then purple. Everyone felt alarmed.

"He's going mad!" whispered Mrs. Plumpy to Miss Skinny.

"Perhaps I put my hanky into my stocking," thought Meddle, in despair. So he pulled up his trouser-ends and felt about in his socks. He took off his shoes, and then his socks, trying to see if the hanky had slipped into the foot. But it wasn't there.

"Meddle! Are you mad?" cried his aunt.

"How can you behave like this?"

Meddle nearly burst himself with trying not to cough or sneeze. "I *did* put my hanky in my vest," he thought. "I know I did. It must have slipped down. I'll take off my coat and waistcoat and see if I can find it."

So, to everyone's horror, Meddle took off his coat and flung it on the floor. Then he took off his waistcoat and that went on the floor, too.

"Poor creature, he is quite mad!" said everyone, and they looked with pity at Meddle's aunt, who was now very red in the face, and felt most ashamed of Meddle.

"This is not the time to undress, Meddle," she said, very sharply.

Meddle was angry. He opened his mouth to say that he was *not* undressing, he was only trying to find his hanky—and, of course, as soon as he opened his mouth the cough and the sneeze came out together.

"A-WHOOSH-OOOOOOOOOOOOOOOO-OO!"

Everyone jumped. Meddle suddenly beamed with delight.

"Here's my hanky!" he said, and he waved it in the air. "It was at the bottom of my vest instead of at the top!"

"Go to the kitchen," said his aunt, angrily. "You are not fit to be here with us. You need to be taught more manners than the little children. I am really ashamed of you, Meddle."

Meddie was surprised. He stared at his

aunt. "But you told me only to sneeze or cough into my hanky," he said, "and I was only trying to find my hanky. You see, I put it in the top of my vest—and it slipped right down to here—and——"

"That will do, Meddle," said his aunt. "We don't want to listen to you. We don't want to see you any more to-day. Carry all these tea-things to the kitchen, and wash up the dishes. That is the least you can do to make up for your very bad behaviour."

Meddle was angry and hurt, but he didn't like to say anything more, when so many people were glaring at him. He had had no tea himself, and he thought it was very hard that no one offered him any.

Meddle finished the washing up and sat and looked at the cakes that were left. He felt hungry. There were plenty of sandwiches left, too.

"Well, I do think I might have a reward for *trying* to sneeze and cough into my hanky, and for washing up the tea-things," he said at last.

So he ate up all the sandwiches, two ginger cakes, three shortbreads, four pieces of sponge-cake, and six chocolate biscuits.

He went home with his aunt later on. "Well," said Meddle, "thanks for taking me, Aunt. I did enjoy the meeting."

But his aunt never knew why, and he didn't tell her! Poor old Meddle, he does his best, but somehow he always makes a muddle, doesn't he!

XIV

YOU'RE A NUISANCE, MISTER MEDDLE!

Once Mister Meddle was going down the lane, past Farmer Corny's apple orchard, when he saw a spire of smoke rising up from the village not far off.

"My!" said Mister Meddle to himself, "that looks as if someone's house is on fire!"

Three small boys came up, and Mister Meddle spoke to them. "Have you come from the village? Is anyone's house on fire?"

"Don't know," said the biggest boy. He turned to look at the spire of smoke. Then he looked at Meddle. Then he looked into the apple orchard, where apples hung ripe and red. He saw there a ladder going up a tree, and at the top of it was Farmer Corny himself, picking apples.

Then the little boy spoke again to Meddle. "Well, maybe there *is* a house

140

on fire!" he said. "Maybe there is someone
that wants rescuing! Maybe they haven't
a ladder to rescue them with! Whatever
will they do?"

Meddle thought it would be fine to be a
hero and rescue someone from a burning
house. He could see himself going up a
long ladder, jumping into a smoky window
and coming out with someone over his

shoulder. How the crowd would cheer him! How grand he would feel!"

"I wish I had a ladder," said Meddle. "You can't rescue people from burning houses without a ladder — —"

"Look, Mister, there's a ladder!" said the naughty little boy, and he pointed to the one in the orchard near by. "You could take that one!"

"So I could, so I could!" said Meddle. "What a sharp little boy you are!"

Meddle jumped over the wall and ran to the ladder. He didn't see the farmer up the tree. He pulled away the ladder and put it over his shoulder.

The farmer saw someone walking off with his ladder and yelled out angrily.

"Hi! Bring that back at once! What do you mean by going off with my ladder?"

"Just going to rescue someone from a burning house!" yelled back Meddle. "I'll bring it back soon. You go on picking your apples!"

The farmer was very angry, but he couldn't get down from the tree because the branches were so high above the ground. The little boys gave Meddle a cheer as he went over the wall with the ladder and set off down the lane. He felt quite a hero already.

The naughty little boys saw the farmer was safely up a high tree and couldn't get down. So up into the smaller trees they went and were soon stuffing their pockets with the rosy-red apples. The farmer went purple with rage, but he couldn't do anything about it. He didn't want to break his leg by jumping down to the ground.

Meddle trotted off down to the village. He met Mr. Jinky and spoke to him.

"Where's the fire?"

"What fire?" said Jinky.

"The house on fire. I'm going to rescue somebody with this ladder," said Meddle. "You know—climb up to a top window."

"Oh," said Jinky. "Well, I should find the fire first if I were you."

Meddle thought that was a silly remark. He went on his way, looking for the fire. But nobody's house seemed to be on fire.

He could still see the spire of smoke rising up in the air, so he went towards it as fast as he could, carrying the heavy ladder over his shoulder.

"Where are you going with that ladder?" asked Dame Trot-About in surprise, when he nearly knocked her over with one end of it.

"Just off to rescue somebody from the burning house!" said Meddle importantly. "Out of my way, please!"

"What burning house?" asked Dame Trot-About in surprise. But Meddle had gone round the corner, almost knocking down a lamp-post with the long ladder!

At last he came to where the smoke rose high in the air. But oh, what a dreadful disappointment for poor Meddle, it was only the smoke from Mr. Smiley's garden bonfire. It was a very, very good bonfire, and the smoke rose high from it. Mr. Smiley was piling all kinds of things on it to make it burn well.

"So there isn't a house on fire after all; and there isn't anyone to rescue!" said poor Meddle sadly. Mr. Smiley thought Meddle must be mad.

"I don't know what you mean," he said. "why are you taking that heavy ladder about?"

Meddle didn't answer. He turned sadly round, almost knocking one of Mr. Smiley's trees down with the end of the ladder, and went back to Farmer Corny's orchard.

As soon as he got there he heard the farmer's angry voice. "You wait till I catch you young monkeys! Stealing my apples like that! You just wait!"

The naughty boys didn't see Meddle coming back with the ladder. Meddle saw at once what had happened, and he put the ladder back up the farmer's tree. Farmer Corny was down in a trice.

Didn't those bad boys get a shock! My goodness me, there was the farmer at the bottom of their tree. And what a shaking and slapping they got when they came down. They had to empty their pockets of the apples and off they went howling.

Then the farmer turned to Meddle, who was standing near by watching. "Good thing I brought the ladder back when I did," said Meddle, thinking that he had done the farmer a good turn.

"What did you want to take it away for?" cried the farmer, and to Meddle's enormous surprise, he found himself caught by the farmer's huge hand and shaken hard—so hard that his teeth rattled in his head, and he was afraid they would fall out!

"*I'll* teach you to take ladders to rescue people!" cried the farmer. "*I'll* teach you to let bad boys get into my trees and steal my apples. *I'll* teach you to leave me stuck up a tree for ages!"

He did teach Meddle—for I'm sure he will never, never take a ladder again and go rushing off to rescue people from a burning house that is only a bonfire.

Poor old Meddle!

XV

MISTER MEDDLE IS RATHER FOOLISH

Once upon a time Mister Meddle went on a walking tour with Mr. Jinks, his friend. They walked all day long in the summer heat, and got rather tired and very hot and extremely cross.

And then Mr. Jinks began to sneeze! Mister Meddle stared at him in amazement.

"Jinks! You don't mean to say you can possibly have caught cold in this hot weather?"

"Well, that's just when you *do* catch cold!" said Jinks, blowing his nose. "You get very hot—and then take off a lot of clothes—and the wind blows, and hey presto—atishoo—a cold has arrived!"

"How very silly!" said Mister Meddle. "Well, come on, Jinks. We'll never get to the next village if we don't hurry! I want something to eat—and then we'll go to bed, bed, bed, and rest our poor tired feet."

"It's a pity we have to use our feet so much on a walking holiday," groaned Mr. Jinks. "I should enjoy walking so much more if I could go on a bicycle."

"Don't be silly," said Meddle.

"That's twice you've said I'm silly," said Jinks crossly. "I wish you'd be quiet if you can't say anything more polite."

"All right," said Meddle. "I won't say another word!"

And he didn't, not even when Jinks asked him a question. So by the time they arrived at the next village and looked for an inn they were not the best of friends.

They found a cosy little inn and went inside. They had a fine supper of ham and eggs, stewed plums, junket and cocoa. After that they both felt so sleepy that they fell asleep in their chairs and didn't wake up till it was dark.

"This *is* silly of us!" groaned Jinks, waking up and yawning. "Come on, Meddle, let's go to bed. A-tish-oo! A-TISH-OO! Oh, bother this cold!"

"I hope you keep it to yourself and don't give it to me," said Meddle. "Hurry up. I've lighted the candle."

They both went upstairs. They had a cosy bedroom with a funny slanting ceiling and a floor that went up and down, it was so uneven.

They undressed and got into bed. "Isn't it hot?" said Meddle. "We'd better open the window."

"Oh no, please don't," said Jinks,

sneezing again. "I shall get a much worse cold if we have an open window with the wind blowing on us all night long."

"But, Jinks, I can't sleep if I'm hot," said Meddle.

"And I can't sleep if I'm cold," said Jinks firmly. "And what's more, I'm JOLLY WELL NOT going to have the window open to-night. Do you want me to be too ill in the morning to go on with our walking?"

"Oh, well, please yourself," said Meddle, getting into bed. "But I tell you this, Jinks, I am QUITE, QUITE SURE that I shan't be able to go to sleep unless the window is open."

They both shut their eyes. Jinks sneezed and coughed. Meddle tossed and turned. He felt hotter and hotter and hotter. It was dreadful! Oh, to have the window open and feel a nice cool breeze blowing! He could go to sleep at once then.

"I'm so dreadfully hot," said Meddle. He breathed very fast to show Jinks how hot he was. "I almost feel that my tongue will hang out like a dog's soon."

"Well, if it does, perhaps you'll stop talking and let *me* get to sleep," said Jinks crossly.

"Jinks! How perfectly horrid you are!" cried Meddle. "Oh dear! I'm so hot I must throw all the clothes off."

"Well, don't throw them off me, too!" said Jinks, clutching at the blankets as Meddle threw them off. "Oh, do lie down and go to sleep. You're just making a fuss. I could easily go to sleep if only you would."

"Well, I tell you that I shall never, never, never go to sleep if we don't have the window open," groaned Meddle.

"Oh, for goodness' sake, open it then," said Jinks crossly. "*I'll* never go to sleep as long as you lie awake throwing all the clothes off me, and tossing about like a whale trying to catch its dinner."

"Don't be silly," said Meddle.

"That's the third time you've said that," said Jinks fiercely, sitting up in bed. "If you say it again I'll throw you out of bed."

"All right, all right," said Meddle, getting out of bed. "I'm going to open the window. Wherever is it?"

"Over there," said Jinks.

"What do you mean, over there?" said Meddle, feeling around. "There's an awful lot of over theres in this room. But there doesn't seem to be any window."

"Of course there is," said Jinks. "Light the candle and find it."

"The candle seems to have disappeared, and the matches, too," said Meddle, feeling about. "Ah—I believe I've got the window now. I can feel glass!"

"I'm sure the window wasn't there," said Jinks, in surprise. "I thought there was a bookcase there or a table or something."

"Well, you thought wrong," said Meddle, fumbling round the glass. "A window is made of glass, isn't it? Well, this is glass, so it's the window. Don't be silly."

"Meddle! I'll kick you out of bed as soon as you get in!" said Jinks furiously.

"Don't worry. I shan't be in for a long, long time yet," said Meddle dolefully. "I can't seem to find out how to open this silly window at all. It just doesn't seem to open at the top or the bottom or the side. Oh, I'm getting so ANGRY with it!"

"Tell it not to be silly," said Jinks.

"Well, I will!" said Meddle, and he spoke angrily to the window. "Don't be silly, window! If you don't let me open you, I'll

154

smash you and let the fresh air in that way!"

But it was no good. Meddle simply could NOT open the window at all. He got angrier and angrier. And to make things worse, Jinks suddenly began to giggle. How he giggled! He went on and on like a river running down hill. Meddle was simply furious with him.

"Now what in the wide world are you giggling about, Jinks?" he said. "Is it so funny that I can't open the window?"

"Yes, Meddle — if you only knew what I know, you'd be giggling, too!" chuckled Jinks, stuffing the sheet into his mouth to stop himself from laughing.

"Well, what *do* you know," asked Meddle, slapping his hand against the glass angrily.

"Shan't tell you," said Jinks. "You keep calling me silly — so I'll *be* silly and not tell you."

"Well, you're sillier than I even thought you were," said Meddle in disgust. "Oh, you awful window! Oh, you horrid thing!

Take that — and that — and that!"

Meddle hit out for all he was worth — and there came the sound of breaking glass!

"Ah!" said Meddle. "I'm glad I've broken you, very glad. You deserved it. Now the fresh air can come in and I can breathe it and go to sleep. Ahhhhh — the lovely fresh air!"

Meddle sniffed and sniffed, thinking how marvellously cool the room had become.

"Don't you feel the lovely fresh air blowing in, Jinks?" he asked.

"No, I don't," said Jinks.

"What! Can't you feel that cool breeze?" cried Meddle, climbing into bed.

"No, I can't," said Jinks, and he gave another giggle.

"I simply don't know what's come over you to-night, Jinks," said Meddle, settling down under the blankets. "Giggling like that over nothing. You ought to be ashamed of yourself."

"*You'll* be ashamed of yourself in the

morning," said Jinks, with another help-
less giggle.

"I certainly shan't," said Meddle. "My
word, it's quite cool now that I've broken
that window and let in the cold night air.
Good night, Jinks. I hope you'll have got
over your giggles by the morning."

Jinks had another fit of giggles, and
shook the bed with them. Meddle shut his
eyes and was soon asleep. And then Jinks
slept too, though once he awoke and began
to giggle again.

In the morning Meddle sat up and
yawned. He stared at the window. It was
fast shut! The glass was not broken at all!

"There's a funny thing!" said Meddle.
"Didn't I break you last night, window?"

Jinks sat up and began to giggle again.
He pointed to a bookcase over in the
corner. It had a glass front to it that was
locked — and some of the glass was
smashed!

"Oh, Meddle! You broke that glass-
fronted bookcase last night and not the
window!" said Jinks, going off into a long

laugh. "I knew you had—that's why I began to giggle. It was so funny the way you kept asking me if I didn't feel the cool air coming in through the broken window —and all the time the window was quite whole and fast shut, and it was the bookcase you had broken!"

"Goodness gracious!" said Meddle, in dismay. "I'll have to pay a lot of money for that. Well, well—how was it I thought I felt the cold night air coming in, I wonder? I just simply can't understand it!"

"I can!" said Jinks, going off into giggles again. "You're just a silly, Meddle—just a GREAT BIG SILLY!"

And for once in a way poor Meddle couldn't find any answer at all!

MISTER MEDDLE AND THE HORSE

Now once Farmer Straw was ill, and he was worried about his horse.

"He needs someone to look after him," he said to his servant girl, Annie. "Send for Meddle. Maybe he can keep an eye on him for me. He will need feeding, and watering, and a little canter over the hills now and again."

So Meddle was sent for and Farmer Straw told him about the horse.

"You keep an eye on him for me," he said. "He is a good, well-mannered horse, and won't be any trouble. He is a wise old fellow, is Captain, and he understands every word you say to him."

"Does he really?" said Meddle, surprised. "Well, I shan't have much difficulty with him, then. Don't you worry, Farmer Straw. Captain and I will get on well together."

"There are oats in the bin," said the farmer. "And the grooming brush is in his stable. You'll have to give him water, too, because the field he is in has no stream running through it."

"Right," said Meddle, and walked off, feeling most important. He had once looked after a canary, and once after his aunt's cat—but he had never looked after such a big animal as a horse before.

"Such a wise old horse, too," thought

Meddle. "Understands every word said to him. Fancy that! Well, I can ask him what he wants, and he'll know all right."

Meddle went to the field where Captain was. The horse cantered over to him.

"Hallo, Captain," said Meddle, and patted his nose. "Do you want a nice drink of water? I can bring you some in a pail, if you do."

"Nay-ay-ay-ay-ay!" neighed the horse, pleased to hear the word "water" for he was thirsty.

"Nay?" said Meddle. "Did you say 'nay'? That means no. So you don't want any water. All right. You really are a clever horse. You not only understand what I say to you, but you answer, too."

Meddle went off to get his dinner. The horse looked after him, disappointed. He wanted some water, but he didn't get it.

After dinner Meddle went back to the horse, which cantered eagerly to the gate.

"Would you like some oats?" asked Meddle.

"Nay-ay-ay-ay-ay!" neighed the horse,

in delight. Oats! Just what he would like! The grass in his field was very poor—but oats were good.

"Nay?" said Meddle, surprised. "Dear me—fancy not wanting oats. I shouldn't have thought a big hefty horse like you would have said 'nay' to oats. I should have thought you would have said 'yes'."

He looked at the horse, who nuzzled against him, trying to let him know that he wanted both oats and water. Meddle stroked his soft nose.

"Would you like to come out of your field for a nice little canter?" he said. "Farmer Straw said you might like a run over the hills."

"Nay-ay-ay-ay-ay!" neighed the horse at once, in delight. Ah—if he could only get out for a canter, he could drink from the first stream he came to. That would be fine.

"What a horse you are for saying no to everything," said Meddle. "Don't you want anything at all, Captain? It's no trouble to me to get you anything you want, you know."

"Nay-ay-ay-ay-ay," said the old horse.

"All right," said Meddle. "If you don't want anything, I won't get it. I'm off to market now. If you're a good horse, maybe I'll bring you back something you'll like."

He set off to market. He bought all kinds of things there for himself—and he bought a beautiful bunch of early carrots for Captain, the horse. They were very dear, very small, but very sweet.

"Aha! Captain will like these," thought Meddle to himself. "He won't say no to these. He'll say 'yes-es-es-es-essssss!'"

He went home with his goods. Then he went to the field, carrying behind him the bunch of feathery carrots. He spoke to Captain, who nuzzled at him eagerly, smelling the carrots that Meddle hid behind his back.

"Captain, do you want some nice young carrots?" asked Meddle. "Now, think before you answer!"

"Nay-ay-ay-ay-ay!" neighed the horse in delight. Carrots! How wonderful. But Meddle was cross.

"There you go—saying no to me again!" he said, angrily. "What a particular horse you are! Nothing I offer you pleases you! You won't have water, oats, a canter or even new carrots! I am disgusted with you. It's nay, nay, nay all the time. Why don't you say yes, yes, yes, for a change?"

He left the poor, hungry, thirsty old horse and went off home. On the way he passed the farmhouse, and the servant girl saw him. "Come in and speak to the master for a minute," she said. "He's fretting about his old horse."

Meddle marched in. The farmer looked at him. "Meddle, have you fed and watered my horse? Have you taken him for a canter?"

"No," said Meddle. "He's a most obstinate horse. He says 'nay-nay-nay' to everything I ask him. What's the use of looking after a horse that says no to everything?"

"Meddle, don't you know a horse can only say 'nay'?" cried the farmer. "Are you cruel, or just stupid? Meddle, come here. I think you need a really good spanking. Come here."

"Nay-ay-ay-ay-ay!" cried Meddle, and you should have seen him run. He went even faster than the old horse. What a silly he is, isn't he?

MISTER MEDDLE TRIES TO BE HELPFUL

Meddle was staying with his Aunt Jemima and she was not very pleased with him. This was not surprising, for Meddle had filled the salt-cellars with sugar, quite by mistake, and had filled the sugar basin with salt. So they had both had porridge and salt, and egg and sugar, for breakfast.

"If only you'd be a bit more helpful instead of doing such silly things," grumbled Aunt Jemima. "My hand just longs to slap you, Meddle, and a very little more silliness from you and I shan't be able to stop my hand from doing what it wants to."

Meddle went as far from his aunt as he could. Her hand was big and hard and strong. "I'm very sorry, Aunt," he said. "But the sugar and salt did look so much alike, you see."

"You didn't think of reading what was on the salt-tin, I suppose?" said Aunt

166

Jemima. "No—don't try to alter the salt and the sugar now—you'll only end in mixing them up together."

Meddle was very glad indeed when his aunt said she was going out to tea that afternoon. She was not a nice person to live with when she was cross.

"I'm going to see Sally Simple in the next village," said Aunt Jemima. "Now, as it's a nice sunny afternoon, you sit out in the garden in the sun. Have tea there if you like, and just keep an eye on the washing on the line to see it doesn't blow away. And do try and be good and sensible, so that I shall feel pleased with you when I come back."

"Oh, yes, Aunt," said Meddle, and he meant it. He waved good-bye to his aunt when she went off in her best coat and bonnet. Then he heaved a big sigh of relief. Now there was no one to scold him for a few hours! He would be so good. He would just show his aunt how good he could be!

"I'll take aunt's rocking-chair out into

the garden," he thought. "It's so comfortable to sit in, and I can rock myself in it whilst I am reading. I'll borrow aunt's library book, too, so that I shan't need to keep her waiting for it when she wants to take it back."

He carried the rocking-chair into the middle of the lawn. He fetched two cushions from the drawing-room. He found his aunt's library book and sat down to read it, rocking himself in the sun. It was lovely.

At four o'clock he felt hungry, so he went indoors and found some scones and buttered them. Then he found a nice new ginger cake and took that out for his tea as well. He made himself some tea in the silver teapot, put a nice clean tray-cloth on the tray, and one on the little table beside the rocking-chair, and then sat down to enjoy his tea.

"Aunt Jemima would be pleased to see me having my tea in such a nice way, with a tray-cloth on, and the silver teapot and all," thought Meddle. "She is always telling me I'm untidy and careless and messy. She just ought to see how well I am behaving this afternoon, when she isn't here to see me!"

He had his tea and enjoyed it, reading all the time. His book was so exciting that he couldn't be bothered to wash up the tea-things and clear everything away just then. He would do that afterwards.

He suddenly felt cold. The sun had gone behind an enormous black cloud. Meddle looked up and a big drop of rain fell on his nose, making him jump.

"Oooh! It's going to rain!" said Meddle, annoyed. "I thought it suddenly felt cold. Poor Aunt Jemima—she will just be coming home, and how wet she will get! Her new bonnet will be soaked. She will probably get an awful cold. Poor Aunt Jemima—no mackintosh, no umbrella!"

Then an idea came into his head and he jumped in delight. "Of course—I'll go and meet her, and I'll take her mackintosh and umbrella with me. How pleased she will be! What a good idea! I can just get to the station in time to meet the home-coming train."

Meddle dashed indoors and found his aunt's big blue mackintosh. He took her enormous red umbrella, and went into the front garden and put it up. Splish splash, pitter-patter, how the rain came down! The drops were huge.

"Dear, dear," said Meddle, running

down the road to the station. "How wet Aunt Jemima would have got if I hadn't thought of taking her mackintosh and umbrella! How pleased she will be with me! I can be very kind and thoughtful when I like!"

The train puffed in as Meddle got to the station. He rushed on to the platform and looked for his aunt to get out of the train. But she didn't get out. She didn't seem to be there at all.

"She must have missed the train!" thought Meddle. "Oh dear, there isn't another one for a whole hour. I'd better wait, because the rain is even heavier now."

So he sat down on the platform and waited. He waited and he waited. The hand of the clock crept all round the figure, and at last the hour was gone. The next train came in and Meddle jumped to his feet. At last!

But dear me, there was no Aunt Jemima on that train, either. It was most puzzling. Meddle didn't know what to do He really couldn't wait any more. Why, it was seven o'clock. Aunt Jemima must be staying the night with Sally Simple. What a waste of time it had been, waiting about in the cold station!

He went out of the station, feeling cross. The rain was still pouring down, and it wetted his legs. There were enormous puddles everywhere now, and Meddle wished he had remembered to change his house slippers for rubber boots. He had rushed out just as he was. "Well, I'll put on Aunt's mackintosh, now she won't want it," he thought. So he put it on, and looked very funny in it, for it came almost down to his big feet, and was much too big for him. He put up the big red umbrella and set off home, grumbling to himself.

He got to the front door, when, to his enormous surprise, it was flung open, and there was his aunt, glaring at him.

"Meddle! Where have you been all this time — and with my mackintosh and umbrella, too. I've been looking for you everywhere. WHERE HAVE YOU BEEN?"

"Oh, aunt—I'm so surprised to see you," said Meddle, and he was.

"I said 'WHERE HAVE YOU BEEN?'" said his aunt, angrily.

"To the station, to meet you!" said poor Meddle. "It began to rain so I thought I'd

173

meet you and take your mackintosh and umbrella for you. I thought you'd be glad to see me at the station."

"What's the sense of meeting the train when you knew I was coming home by bus?" snorted his aunt. And then Meddle suddenly remembered that his aunt always went by bus to Sally Simple's and back, because it passed her door and Sally's too!

"Oh, dear me," he said, and felt very silly.

"I should think it *is* 'oh dear me!'" said Aunt Jemima, in a horrid sort of voice. "That's what I said when I jumped off the bus outside the door, ran in—and found you had left all my nice washing out on the line to get wet. It's soaking now—and the mud has splashed up from the ground and made it all dirty again! Why didn't you take it in when it rained?"

"Well, dear me," said Meddle, feeling very awkward about it. "Yes, I should have done that, of course."

"And why did you *have* to leave my best rocking-chair, and my two nice drawing-

room cushions out in the rain, too?"
inquired his aunt. "Did you have to leave
out my silver tea-things—*and* the rest of
the ginger-cake, which is now nothing but
wet crumbs?"

"Good gracious me!" said Meddle, feeling even more uncomfortable.

"And I suppose you thought it was a *very*
good idea to leave my library book out in
the pouring rain, too?" said Aunt Jemima,
her voice getting louder and louder, and
her face getting redder and redder.

Meddle began to feel alarmed. Had he
really done all that? And he had meant to
be so good and helpful.

"Well," he said, "well, Aunt, I *did* take
your mackintosh and umbrella to the
station for you."

"So clever," said his aunt, "so clever!
When I got home and wanted to go and
take in my washing and the tea-things and
chair and cushions and book, I looked for
my mackintosh and umbrella to keep me
dry—but no, they were gone. You had
taken them to put on somebody who wasn't

there, and *you* kept nice and dry while I got soaking wet going out into the garden! Meddle, my hand is longing to slap you!"

"Ooh!" said Meddle, and ran straight out into the garden, mackintosh, umbrella and all.

"I can wait till you come in!" called his aunt. "I'll warm you up nicely then. I can wait!"

Poor Meddle. He meant so well, didn't he? He's still out there in the rain, but he'll have to go indoors some time—and then what a spanking he will get!

XVIII

MISTER MEDDLE GETS A SHOCK

Once it happened that Mister Meddle had a whole pound sent him for his birthday. He was so surprised and delighted that he simply didn't know what to do.

"I think I really must go round to my friend Jinky and tell him about it," said Mister Meddle. "Perhaps he will have some good ideas what to spend it on."

So off to Jinky's he went. He showed him the pound-note and told him that it was worth twenty whole shillings.

"But I can't think what to spend it on, Jinky," said Meddle.

"Well, I can tell you!" said Jinky. "You want a new tie and a new coat, a new pair of stockings and a new handkerchief. Why don't you buy those?"

"Can I get all that for twenty shillings?" asked Meddle, very pleased. "Oh, that would be fine! Shouldn't I feel grand!"

"I'll come and help you to buy them,"

said Jinky, and he got up and the two of them went off to the shop.

Well, you should have seen Meddle when he came out! He had on a new red coat, a yellow tie, a pair of blue stockings, and a green-spotted handkerchief! He felt so grand that he could hardly walk!

"Do you feel too grand to walk along with me?" asked Jinky.

"Well, it's a pity you've got such old clothes on — but I'll walk a little way," said Meddle grandly. "Is my tie straight, Jinky? Does my handkerchief show enough? Are my stockings pulled up straight? Dear me, I wish I could meet the King to-day. I guess he'd wonder who I was."

Meddle walked along the road, his nose in the air, stepping out in a very important manner. Jinky ran beside him, wishing that he, too, had some new clothes.

"If I met the King I would bow like this," said Meddle, bowing very suddenly just as an old lady was passing. She looked very startled. "And I would hold out my hand like this, and say, 'How do you do, Your Majesty? It is a pleasure to meet you.' "

The old lady scuttled away, thinking that Meddle must be quite mad.

Meddle walked along again, talking. "And then the King would say to me, 'Ah, how do you do, Meddle? How grand you are looking to-day! Wherever do you buy such beautiful clothes?' "

"Mind where you are walking, Meddle," said Jinky anxiously, seeing that they were coming to where a dirty old coal-cart was standing near the pavement.

"Don't interrrupt me, Jinky," said Meddle crossly. "As I was saying, the King would want to know where I got such fine clothes. And I would say, 'Your Majesty, come with me and I will buy you a handkerchief just like mine.' And the King would say, 'No, Meddle—you come with *me*. Just step into my carriage, my dear fellow.' And I would step into his carriage like this . . ."

Meddle had got his nose so high in the air that he didn't see he was passing an open coal-hole, down which the coalman had been emptying coal into a cellar. He stepped right into the hole, and fell down into black darkness!

"This isn't the King's carriage!" said Meddle in surprise. "Where am I? I was just stepping into a carriage—and now I'm here, in a dark, dirty prison!"

Jinky hadn't seen Meddle step into the

coal-hole, for he was a little way in front. He turned round to speak to Meddle—and, dear me, Meddle wasn't there! He just simply wasn't there! The only person in the street was a coalman just emptying a sack of coal down a coal-hole!

"Good gracious!" said Jinky, most surprised. "Where has Meddle gone? He has simply vanished into thin air! What a very extraordinary thing!"

Jinky hurried on to see if by any chance Meddle had got in front of him—and round the corner what should he meet but the King's carriage, with the King himself inside!

"Look at that now!" said Jinky, astonished. "The King and his carriage! Meddle wanted to meet them—and now's his chance. Meddle! Meddle! Where are you? Here's the King!"

Meddle was down the coal-hole, of course —and a sack of coal had just been emptied on to his surprised head! He was covered in coal-dust from head to foot! Poor old Meddle!

When the coal came tumbling down, Meddle was very angry. "Stop it!" he cried. "Stop throwing stones at me! Who is it treating me like this? Wait till I get hold of you!"

That was the last sack of coal. The coalman went back to his cart with his sack. And at that moment Jinky came along crying, "Meddle! Meddle! Here's the King!"

Meddle looked up and saw the open coalhole above him. He began to climb out, eager to see the King. But when Jinky saw a black-faced creature appearing suddenly at his feet, he was full of terror. He turned and fled, shouting, "A black-faced monster! A black-faced monster!"

Meddle thought Jinky had gone mad. He climbed out just as the King's carriage came rolling by. Up stepped Meddle and took off his hat. He held out his coal-black hand. "How do you do, Your Majesty?" he said in a very grand and polite tone.

But the King didn't answer as he ought to have done. He stared coldly at Meddle and said, "Who is this dirty beggar? Go home and have a bath, man, and don't dare to appear in the streets like that."

And the carriage drove on, leaving Meddle staring after it, puzzled and hurt. He set off home, wondering what the matter was. He didn't know he was covered with coal-dust. He thought that he looked as grand as ever, in his new blue coat, tie, handkerchief and stockings!

He came to Jinky's house and went in to see what had happened to his friend. But when Jinky opened the door and saw the black-faced creature standing there, he fled away to his kitchen in a fright.

"He's after me, he's after me!" squealed poor Jinky.

"Who's after you?" called Meddle in astonishment, and he went to see. In the hall was a long mirror, and for the first time Meddle saw himself all black. He didn't know he was looking at himself, and he stared in horror.

"He's after me, too," yelled Meddle, and he tore out of the house and went home as fast as ever he could. And then, when he saw his own face looking at him out of his glass at home, quite black, he knew what had happened!

"I fell down a coal-hole," groaned Meddle. "I was feeling too high and mighty—and I fell down the coal-hole. It serves me right. What *must* the King think of me? Oh dear, oh dear—he'll never, never ask me to ride in his carriage now! Never, never!"

And Meddle was right. The King certainly never did!

Also by Enid Blyton

MR MEDDLE'S MISCHIEF

"You're a tiresome, meddlesome creature, Mister Meddle!"

Mr Meddle is a very silly pixie. He's always getting in a muddle. He washes his hair with sherbet and cleans his teeth with glue; he feeds cake mixture to the pigs and worms to the budgies; he meddles with a conjuror's magic and drives an engine into the river. He just can't keep out of trouble!

Enid Blyton

SNOWBALL THE PONY

"There he is! Oh, isn't he sweet? He's the nicest little pony we've ever seen!"

Snowball is scared when he learns that he's going to live with a new family, leaving his mother behind. But he has only been sold to the next-door farm, and the three children who live there treat him well, and he soon settles down happily. He has lots of adventures; he gives the children rides, gets chased by an old sow, and teaches a naughty boy a lesson!

Enid Blyton

THE SAUCY JANE FAMILY

"Welcome to the Saucy Jane!"

Mike, Belinda and Ann spend their holidays on a beautiful houseboat on the canal – and what an exciting time they have! They learn to swim and have some wonderful holiday treats – like taking a trip on a real canal boat.

Enid Blyton

THE SEASIDE FAMILY

They were off – off to Sea-gull Cove by the sea!

Mike, Belinda and Ann are going on a seaside holiday. What's more, they are taking their home with them – it's easy when you live in a caravan! And what a wonderful summer lies ahead, with the sea right outside their door!

Enid Blyton

THE MAGIC FARAWAY TREE

"Oh, do let's take our lunch up into the Land of Topsy-Turvy. Oh, do, do!"

Dick thought it would be dull in the country with Jo, Bessie and Fanny. But that was before he found the magic Faraway Tree! The four children have the most extraordinary adventures with the Saucepan Man, Moon-Face and Silky the elf. They only have to climb through the cloud at the top of the huge tree to be in the Land of Spells, or Land of Topsy-Turvy, or even the Land of Do-As-You-Please!

Jo, Bessie and Fanny go on more exciting escapades in *The Enchanted Wood* and *The Folk of the Faraway Tree*.

Enid Blyton

THE FOLK OF THE FARAWAY TREE

"A land at the top of a tree!" said Connie. "I don't believe a word of it."

Jo, Bessie and Fanny are fed up when Connie comes to stay – she's so stuck-up and bossy. But they don't let her stop them having fun with their tree-friends, Silky, Moon-Face and the Saucepan Man. Together they climb through the cloud at the top of the Faraway Tree and visit the wonderful places there, the Land of Secrets and the Land of Treats – and Connie learns to behave herself!

Jo, Bessie and Fanny have more magical adventures in *The Enchanted Wood* and *The Magic Faraway Tree*.

Other Enid Blyton titles available from Mammoth